SCROLLS FROM THE ARCHIVES

A Fire & Brimstone Short Story Collection

Nikole Knight

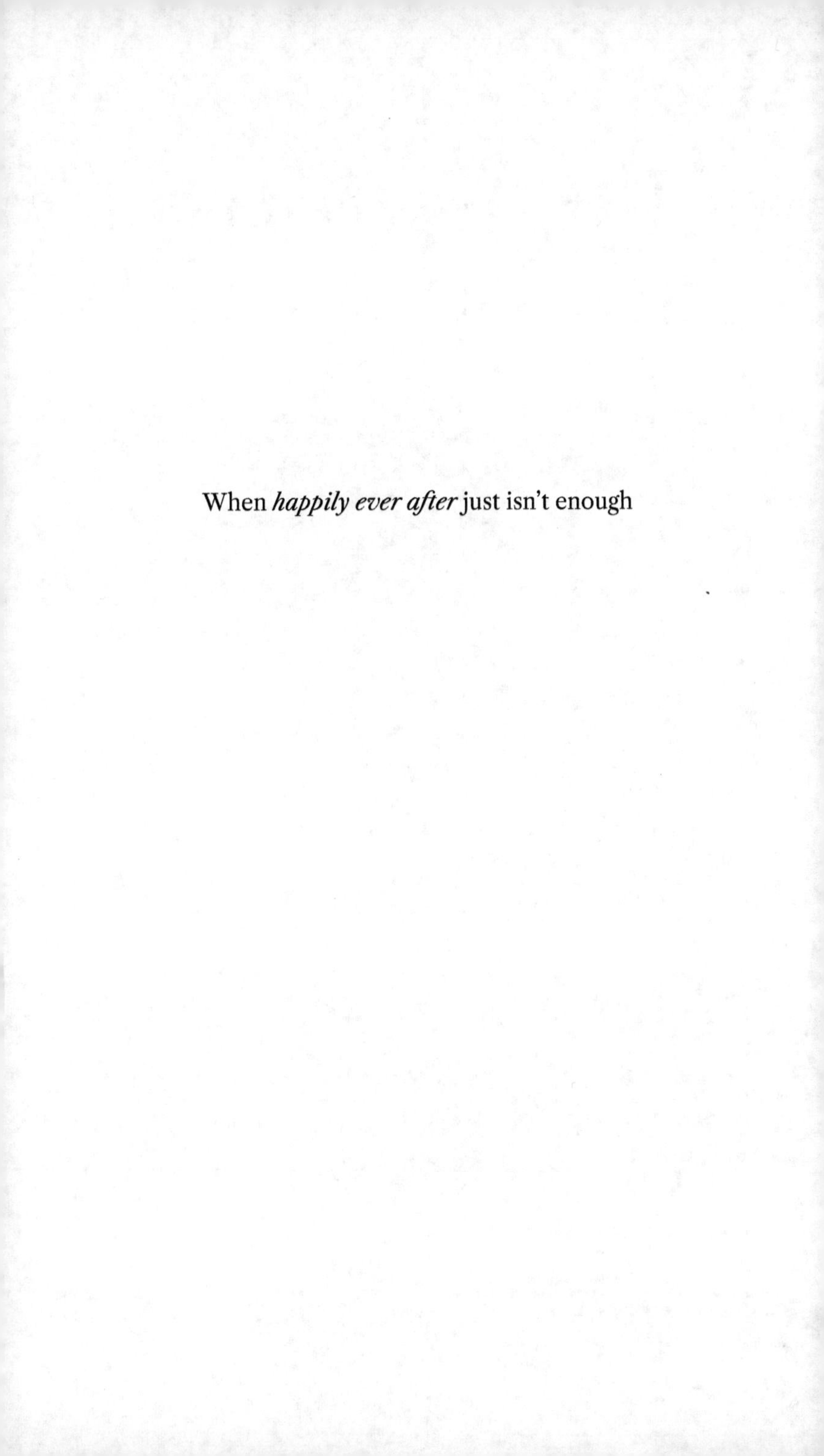

When *happily ever after* just isn't enough

OTHERS

PART ONE

Jai

RILEY'S LAUGHTER FILTERED THROUGH the house, and Jai paused at the bottom of the stairs to listen. Sweet aromas drifted from the kitchen where Gideon and Riley were baking cookies. Well, they were supposed to be baking cookies. Judging from Riley's soft sigh and the quiet, wet sound of a kiss, they were doing everything but baking.

Unable to help himself, Jai snuck to the kitchen archway and peeked inside. The air was warm from the oven, but it was the sight before him that sent heat zipping down his spine. Riley sat on the counter next to a bowl of cookie dough, legs dangling on either side of Gideon's hips. Gideon cradled Riley's face gently in his hands as their noses brushed.

Riley held his index finger to Gideon's mouth, a dollop of cookie dough piled there. Chuckling, Gideon accepted the bite, and Riley blushed beautifully. Then Gideon pressed a sweet kiss to Riley's lips, and their boy melted with another contented sigh.

Feeling guilty for creeping on them, Jai backed quietly away. Riley's arousal was a dull buzz in the background of their Committed bond, and Jai closed the connection from his end. The rope pulsed, a subtle question from his Committed. He squeezed back in reassurance, and Riley faded away once more, his focus returning to Gideon.

Gideon and Riley spent a lot of time together, but it was rare for them to share physical intimacy. Rarer still was catching them in the act. It was sickeningly adorable, but Jai knew it wasn't for his eyes. Letting them be, he climbed the stairs to his bedroom.

The quiet murmur of Noel's TV droned from his room, and Jai didn't think twice about entering without knocking. Noel yelped, turning away from his full-length mirror to face Jai. He crossed his arms over his body like he was trying to cover himself, but it made no difference. Jai could see every inch of the sundress draping Noel's frame.

"Uh," Jai said, and Noel's wide eyes took on a glassy sheen.

"I was just…" he drifted off, his expression crumpling as his breath hitched. "I was—"

"Hey, it's okay." Jai shut the door and turned the lock in case Riley and Gideon came upstairs. Then he faced his Other again. "You don't have to explain."

"It's not what it looks like," Noel said.

Jai arched an eyebrow. "So you're not trying on a sundress in secret?"

Cringing, Noel hugged himself tighter. His cheeks flamed red, and embarrassment and fear strangled the bond pulsing between them. "Okay, it's exactly what it looks like."

Cautiously, Jai stepped toward his Other, trying to catch his wandering, amethyst gaze. "Noel?"

"Go on then," Noel snapped, glaring at the carpet. "Make your jokes. Call me a girl or whatever."

Noel's chin quivered, and Jai's heart cracked down the middle. Jai had always been gruff, blunt, and more than a little harsh, but Noel gave as much as he got. They teased each other; they poked and prodded. It was how they'd always been. Sure, Jai went too far sometimes, but he never realized how deep his words had embedded themselves in his Other, how they'd festered there like an infected wound, even after all these years of loving each other without restraint.

Hades, how had he never noticed what a fucking asshole he was?

"Why would I do that?" he said, taking another careful step.

Like a wary animal, Noel matched his movement with a step backward of his own. "Why not? I look ridiculous."

Jai observed him again, taking in the pastel blue fabric teasing Noel's legs at mid-thigh, the way it bunched high on his waist. The material sagged at his chest because, well, he didn't have breasts to fill it. But the color was soft against his pale complexion, making his eyes look more blue than purple.

"It's nice," Jai said.

Noel's light brows rose in disbelief. "Fuck you, Jairus."

"I'm serious."

With a scoff, Noel turned away from him, facing the mirror once more.

Jai could see the sheen of tears in his Other's reflection, and it made his ruined heart ache. "It's pretty, Noel."

"It fits all wrong."

Slowly, Jai approached until he was close enough to touch the cotton fabric looped around Noel's neck. He bundled Noel's hair and gently twisted it, draping it over the front of his shoulder. Then he gathered the loose strap of the halter and pulled until the top of the dress was flat against Noel's chest.

"Where did you buy it?" Jai asked.

Noel chewed his bottom lip before answering. "At a boutique in the earthly realm."

"Well," Jai began—carefully, carefully. "It was designed for cis females. So it won't fit right unless you adjust it. Tighten the strap." He met Noel's gaze in the mirror. "I hate to break it to you, but you don't have boobs."

That earned a wobbly smile and a wet laugh from Noel. "Thank the Maker."

Jai grinned. "If you bring it in here and here"—he tugged and pinched the material at Noel's waist and neck—"it will fit more naturally. See?"

Their gazes clashed again, and Noel nodded jerkily. "Yeah, I guess."

"It's a nice color on you."

"You think so?"

With a nod, Jai rubbed Noel's bare arms. "Yeah. You look really pretty."

"But I shouldn't, right?" He smoothed his hands down his front. "I'm a warrior. A Guardian. I'm not supposed to want to feel pretty."

"Bullshit! You're fucking perfect the way you are, whether you wear fatigues or evening gowns," Jai growled, fingers tightening on Noel's biceps. "And I'll gut anyone who tells you different."

"Always the protector," he mused, and Jai eased his grip, not wanting to bruise Noel's porcelain skin.

"You're my Other. No one gives you shit but me."

Noel laughed, the sound like twinkling windchimes. "And you're not giving me shit for this?"

"Maybe, because you should've told me sooner," Jai grumbled.

"I never let myself explore it, so how could I have talked to you about it?" Noel cocked his head. "I was never like you, Jairus. I was always smaller, prettier, more delicate. I had to prove my masculinity. Wearing something like this would have negated everything I fought so hard for, all the respect I earned through my blood and sweat."

His eyes were dark purple now, his jaw clenched. Jai leaned down and pressed a kiss to Noel's shoulder. "I'm sorry."

"It's not your fault. People look at me, and they see a pretty twink, a weak little queen who needs protecting." Noel's shoulders slumped. "I just had to try harder than you did to prove them wrong, and it took me a long time to accept the parts of myself that I'd hidden away. Like wanting to feel and look pretty."

Slipping his arms around Noel's waist, Jai hugged him close, burying his face in a neck smelling of lilac and sunshine. "You've always been strong and fierce and brave. You never had to prove that to *me*. You know that, right?"

"I know."

Unable to look Noel in the eyes, Jai nuzzled his shoulder, choosing his words wisely. "Is there more to this than the clothes?"

Noel turned in his hold, hands coming to rest on Jai's chest. He frowned. "What—"

"You can tell me anything, and it wouldn't change how I see you, how I feel about you," Jai insisted, needing Noel to believe him. "I love you, okay? No matter what."

The most tender expression flooded Noel's face as he cupped Jai's bearded cheeks. "I know. I love you too. It's not about gender, if that's what you're asking. I like who I am, on the inside and on the outside. I just like the way I feel when I'm wearing something like this."

Jai traced the zipper lying along Noel's spine. "I like how you look wearing something like this."

Noel blushed. "Thank you."

"Does Riley know?"

"Maybe. I, uh, wear nighties sometimes, lace and stuff." Noel shrugged, and irrational jealousy speared through Jai's chest. Not against Noel for having Riley, but for Riley seeing Noel in something so lovely and delicate. They'd been sharing Riley for almost five years now, and envy cropped up every now and then. But feeling jealous of *Riley* was rather new.

Noel and Jai's relationship was ever-changing, evolving with every new challenge and experience they shared. They fucked around with Riley at least once a week, if not more, but they never fucked just the two of them. With Riley in the middle, it made sense. They focused on his pleasure, first and foremost, and touching each other was simply a byproduct.

They'd kissed, jerked each other off, and gone down on each other because it turned Riley on to watch. Sure, Jai enjoyed everything they did together, and driving Noel crazy by eating out his ass as Riley sucked him off or rode him was hot as fuck. But again, Riley was always there, the instigator, the spark igniting the flame.

And yet the idea of Noel wearing lingerie for Riley but not for *him* colored Jai green with envy.

"Jai?" Noel curled a hand around the back of his neck, squeezing lightly. "What—"

"You should tell Riley," Jai said, clearing his throat. "He loves you, and he'll love *this*"—he yanked gently on the dress—"too. You'll see."

"I know. I'll tell him. I just..." Noel bit his bottom lip and grimaced. "This is the first time I've actually put on a dress."

"Really?" Jai asked, and Noel nodded. "So I'm the first one to see, the first one you've told?"

Another nod. Jai's chest swelled with pride, and Noel rolled his eyes. "Don't look so damn pleased with yourself."

"I'll be pleased with myself if I want," Jai muttered, and Noel smacked his chest with a laugh.

Drawing Noel into an embrace, Jai kissed his temple and cradled his Other close. Noel sighed and melted into the hold, arms looped loosely around Jai's neck. They stood that way for a long time, Jai rubbing his hands up and down Noel's back.

"So, those nighties you like to wear..." Jai prompted.

Noel shook with laughter in his arms. "You want me to wear one next time?"

"I've always liked a boy in lace."

"Does Riley wear lace for you?"

Jai thought back to the times Riley had, indeed, dressed up for him. Riley didn't do it too often, mostly because it wasn't his kink and he didn't really get anything out of it other than knowing Jai enjoyed it. But Riley had always been one to accommodate, and when he found out wearing more femme items of clothing drove Jai batshit crazy, he used it to his advantage, the little minx.

"Sometimes," Jai admitted, shifting to add some distance between him and his Other before Noel felt the half-chub hardening in his jeans. "It's not really his thing, though."

"Well, it is my thing, so..."

Noel leaned back far enough to make eye contact, but they were still close. Jai traced the swell of his Other's cheek with his thumb, and Noel smiled.

"You can wear what you want to wear anytime, even with me. Okay?" Jai said, and Noel nodded.

"Okay." Leaning in, Noel pressed a chaste kiss to Jai's lips. "Thank you."

Their breath mingled, and Jai's fingers clenched around the excess fabric at Noel's hips. "You know I got you. No matter what."

"I do. That's why I left the door unlocked," Noel whispered, eyes downcast.

"You wanted me to come in?" Jai nudged Noel's nose with his, but Noel refused to look away from the dip in Jai's throat.

"Maybe."

Noel, whether subconsciously or not, had wanted to share this with Jai, and it made Jai ache. Noel was his *Other*, his partner, the other half of himself, and knowing Noel trusted him enough to be this vulnerable was a heady thing. Maker, it made Jai feel fucking invicible.

"I love you," Jai muttered, clacking his tongue piercing against the back of his teeth.

Finally, Noel lifted his colorless gaze. "I love you too."

Their foreheads met as they breathed each other's air. Jai's hands rubbed up and down Noel's sides, fingers dragging over sleek muscle and hard bone. Until his pinkie slipped lower, catching on something thick at Noel's hip underneath his dress.

Curving his hand around Noel's hip, he dug his fingers in, feeling rough material beneath the cotton dress. His half-hard cock sprang to life with a force he wasn't prepared for, and Noel yelped as Jai dropped both hands to cup Noel's ass.

"Jai!" he squeaked.

"Holy fuck, you're wearing panties!" Jai accused.

Noel blushed deeply. "I'm in a dress. I can't exactly wear boxers underneath."

With a shudder, Jai snuck a hand under the hem of Noel's dress, teasing the swell of his soft skin where it met rough lace. He groaned. "Fuck, Noel."

Stumbling back a few steps, he raked a hand through his hair and shook his head. His thoughts clouded as desire roared through his veins. Because Noel was standing in front of him, flushed and beautiful and wearing fucking lace panties!

Maker in Heaven, Jai had never wanted Noel more.

OTHERS

PART TWO

Noel

NOEL FURROWED HIS BROWS as Jai scrubbed a palm down his face. His dark eyes ignited with fire, and his nostrils flared. Arousal pinged through their bond, and Noel nearly jolted from the unexpected force of it.

Sure, they'd fucked each other in different ways whenever they had a threesome with Riley, but they'd never fully pursued sex with just the two of them. Their desire for each other was like a pot that forever simmered on the backburner, only reaching a boil when they dropped the pretense in Riley's presence.

But Riley wasn't here. It was just Noel, and Jai was staring at him like he was starving and Noel was a five-course meal.

With a sly grin, Noel touched the hem of his sundress. "Do you like that I'm wearing panties, Jai?"

"Noel." Jai growled a warning, and a delightful shiver snaked down Noel's spine.

Riley had asked Noel more times than he could count why he and Jai had yet to fuck, just the two of them. Noel never had a good answer for it. Fear of ruining the relationship, possibly?

They had a good dynamic, and neither of them wanted to fuck it up for something as inconsequential as sex. Even though they'd spent the last five years in a polyamorous relationship, sharing Riley with each other and their Prime, they had danced around that final line drawn in the sand.

But they were on the cusp of something. Here. Now. At last.

"Jairus," Noel cooed, stepping toward his Other.

"Noel."

One more step. "Do you love me?"

Jai said, "Yes."

Another step. "Do you want me?"

Jai said, "*Yes*."

The last step. "Then kiss me."

And Jai kissed him. It was a hard kiss, but Noel expected nothing less from his Other. Jai's lips were demanding, unyielding. His callused hands grasped. His beard scraped against Noel's chin as his tongue plunged into his mouth.

Jai pulled. Noel pushed.

Backing Noel against the wall, Jai boxed him in, devouring him, but Noel gave as good as he got. He was hard as steel, his erection straining the delicate lace beneath his dress. He felt Jai's arousal through his jeans, and he whimpered into Jai's mouth. He needed more.

When Jai's hands gripped his thighs and heaved, Noel jumped, wrapping his legs around Jai's waist. Those hands—Maker, those hands. They burned every inch of

Noel's skin as they slid higher, cupping his ass. Jai groaned against Noel's lips, his fingers flexing on the lace.

Noel pushed. Jai pulled.

Noel fisted a hand in Jai's hair as the other slipped under his shirt, tracing toned, trembling muscle. Jai had always been exquisite. He'd trained hard and been rewarded with a body Noel wanted to run his tongue over. For now, he would settle for tracing every dip and valley of Jai's torso with his fingertips.

He knew exactly what Jai looked like, had every inch of his body memorized. They'd been together for centuries after all, and while Noel had never allowed himself to harbor ideas of touching or *taking*, he'd looked. How could he not? He may not have been human, but he was a man.

Yes, he knew everything there was to know about Jai, about the way his body moved, how it felt. He'd witnessed the ferocity of him as Jai fought, the grace of him as he put words to his emotion through music, the softness of him as he made love to their Riley, deep and slow.

But this was the first time Noel had ever explored Jai this way. It was the first time he had ever made Jai tremble. Every grunt and moan was for Noel and Noel alone.

"Noel," Jai rasped against his neck, hauling the cotton sundress up, up, up and over Noel's head. "Noel, what do you want? You need to tell me what you want, *neshama sheli*."

"You." Noel cupped his bearded face and ground his hard cock against Jai's stomach. "Just you."

"Are you sure? I need you to—"

Noel cut off his chivalrous courtesy with a kiss, fucking Jai's mouth with his tongue. "I'm sure. I want this."

"With me?" The uncharacteristic insecurity in Jai's voice nearly broke Noel's heart.

"With you, *chaim sheli*," Noel assured him with tender kisses and kind touches, and oh, how Jai *smiled*.

The next kiss was sweet and slow, and when Jai turned and carried Noel toward the bed, Noel shuddered with pleasure and anticipation. The TV mounted on the wall droned quietly, but he couldn't remember where he'd left the remote. Jai didn't seem bothered by the background noise, so Noel put it out of his mind as his back met the mattress.

Noel tugged on Jai's shirt and somehow managed to yank it off as Jai struggled to unbuckle his belt at the same time. "Would you hold your horses?" Jai complained as Noel wrenched his arm at an awkward angle in an attempt to remove his shirt completely. "Ow!"

"Sorry," Noel said around a laugh. "I just don't think it's fair that I'm naked and you're fully clothed."

With a sinister smile, Jai snapped the waistband of Noel's panties. "You're not entirely naked yet."

"Take off your pants," Noel ordered, and it was Jai's turn to laugh.

"Yes, your highness," he sassed as he stood at the end of the bed between Noel's knees. He unfastened his jeans, then shoved them down, underwear and all. His erection was long, and the tip peaked out from his foreskin, flushed and a little purple with desperation.

Noel circled his fingers around Jai's cock and peeled back the foreskin, revealing his frenum piercing. With a sly smirk up at his Other, Noel leaned in and licked around the head of his cock, playing with the warm metal balls of the piercing. Jai groaned, a gentle hand cupping Noel's cheek.

When Jai's fingers sifted through Noel's hair, Noel breathed through the fleeting moment of fear. It had been years since Noel had been locked in that dank dungeon, forced to his knees or fucked against his will, but some triggers held strong.

But Jai knew, and he would never hurt Noel. His fingers were so gentle, petting and caressing instead of yanking and tearing. Noel relaxed, parting his lips to suck the plump head of Jai's cock into his mouth. He was rewarded with a bitter pearl of precum.

"You're so fucking gorgeous," his Other said reverently, and Noel smiled around Jai's cock, swallowing him down.

Callused fingers circled Noel's throat, pressing just hard enough to feel the cock he fought not to choke on. A shudder racked Jai, and the pressure on Noel's throat loosened. Lifting off Jai's cock, Noel stroked him with a hand as he nuzzled Jai's stomach.

"Lube?"

"Yes, please," Noel said sweetly, and Jai rolled his eyes.

Stepping away, Jai rifled in Noel's drawer, and Noel scooted back on the bed, nerves and excitement fluttering in his belly. Jai brandished a tube of lube and shut the drawer firmly, his eyes burning. Nonchalantly, Noel leaned against his headboard and traced his laced-covered cock with his index finger.

Like a jungle cat, Jai crawled over the mattress until he was straddling Noel's legs. He batted Noel's hand away and glided a knuckle down Noel's length. Noel bit his bottom lip, his legs twitching under Jai's weight.

"I like these," Jai mused, and Noel looked down, admiring the bright color against his pale, leaking cock. Jai's hand was so dark in contrast to Noel's skin, and goosebumps exploded over his body as Jai drew the panties down just far enough to tuck under Noel's sack. "You're gonna fuck me with these on," he said sternly, and Noels brain glitched.

"Uh, what?"

Jai's hand was too dry as he jacked Noel lazily, an infuriating smirk on his face. "I gotta make good on a promise I made you, don't I?"

It took Noel several seconds to remember what Jai was talking about. "The drunken promise you made four years ago?"

Jai shrugged. "I like to think I'm a man of my word."

"You don't like bottoming," Noel insisted, and his Other's jaw ticked.

"It's not my preference, but it's not like I hate it. If Riley asked, I'd let him top me. He just never asks."

Noel arched a chiding eyebrow. "I wonder why. Riley doesn't ask for anything, especially if he already has it in his head that you won't want it or like it. You'll have to offer, at least the first time."

With a scoff, Jai shook his head. "You're right. I'm a selfish asshole, apparently."

"He's a good top." Noel ran his hands over Jai's abs and through his chest hair. "He'll make it good for you. And you can still... be bossy and stuff."

Jai's snort sent heat rushing to Noel's cheeks. "Bossy?"

"I know you two have a certain dynamic. I'm just saying, you can still be in control, even if you're the one taking it."

"Are you offering?" The words were husky and rough, and Noel met Jai's gaze.

"I'm not submissive, darling," Noel warned, and Jai laughed.

"Oh, I'm aware." Shoving the lube into Noel's hand, he scooted up until he captured both their cocks in his hand. "Now stop talking and fuck me before I change my mind."

"Don't worry. I'll be gentle," Noel cooed, and Jai's responding kiss was biting.

"Not too gentle," he rasped, and Noel shivered.

Jai liked rough sex, but Noel knew Jai hadn't bottomed in years, possibly decades. And he wanted this to be good for them both. So he prepped him carefully as Jai jacked them off. The pressure wasn't enough to make them come, but it kept them hard as Noel stretched his Other.

They were both breathless and sweaty by the time Jai growled against Noel's lips. "I'm not breakable, damn it. I'm ready."

"Don't wanna hurt you," Noel said as he wiped his fingers on the duvet.

"You're not that big," Jai teased, and Noel pinched his nipple. "Ow!"

"Once I'm in your ass, you'll feel differently."

Laughing, Jai lifted up on his knees as Noel slicked his cock. The panties were stretched tight, pushing on the underside of his balls. He was going to fuck Jai with his panties still on. It was hot as Hades.

"You're sure?" Noel checked in once more, and Jai answered by grabbing Noel's dick roughly and positioning it at his ass. "Jai, don't—"

"You won't break me," he growled as he sat back, forcing the head of Noel's cock past the first ring of muscles.

He went faster than Noel would have liked, but Noel trusted Jai to know his own body. And as much as he could, he wanted to offer Jai control. He couldn't submit the way Riley could, but hopefully this was enough.

The tight heat of him nearly sent Noel over the edge, but he held his orgasm back as Jai sank down on Noel's desperate cock. Jai gritted his teeth, his face screwing up in discomfort, and Noel cupped his bearded cheeks and tugged him into a sloppy kiss.

"Slow down," Noel instructed, and Jai grunted.

"I'm fine."

"Jairus."

"Fuck, when did your cock get so big?"

Noel burst into laughter, and Jai half-grinned, half-grimaced. They shared intimate laughter as Jai settled in Noel's lap, ass on his thighs. Sweat beaded Jai's forehead, and Noel kissed his cheeks and lips, rubbing his hands up and down Jai's arms.

"It's been so long. I'd forgotten..." Jai pressed his forehead to Noel's. "It's a lot."

"We can—"

"No, I'm good. I just need a minute."

Noel continued to pet Jai in comfort, waiting for his trembling body to relax. "Take as many minutes as you need. My huge cock can wait."

The attempt at humor broke Jai's tension, and he laughed again. "I never said huge."

Whatever Noel was going to say was cut off by Jai's mouth. His tongue was insistent and rough, his lips almost harsh. His beard was going to leave marks, and Noel loved every second of it.

"Jai," Noel moaned as Jai began to rock. "Maker in Heaven, you feel good."

"So does your huge cock." Jai nipped at Noel's earlobe as Noel gasped out a laugh. "Now let me fuck myself on it."

"Your mouth is sinful." Noel tangled his fingers in Jai's hair and kissed him. It was messy and wet and dirty.

Noel had seen Jai fuck a thousand times, so he knew his Other was capable of more grace than he was currently exhibiting. But he didn't judge Jai for his lack of finesse as he rocked and bounced on Noel's cock.

"How do you and Riley make this look so easy?" Jai griped as his brow furrowed in frustration.

"Practice makes perfect," Noel teased into Jai's facial hair. He framed Jai's hips to help guide him. "Don't fret. We'll find your prostate."

Jai snorted. "At this rate, I'm questioning if I even have one."

Chuckling under his breath, Noel grabbed Jai around the waist and spun them until Jai landed on his back with a grunt. Jai gaped up at Noel with wide eyes, and Noel smiled in reassurance, running fingers through Jai's thick, dark leg hair. With a firm grip under Jai's knee, Noel pushed his leg up until it pressed against his chest.

"You have a prostate, I promise. And I'm going to find it." Noel gave an experimental thrust into Jai's tense body, and Jai's breath punched from his chest. "Now relax and let me make you feel good."

"I am not as flexible as you!" Jai warned, and Noel rolled his eyes.

"Stop whining."

Hooking Jai's leg over his shoulder, Noel leaned in and kissed Jai's grumbled response from his lips. Then he set a steady rhythm, snapping his hips forward until the room filled with the slap of skin and heavy grunts. Jai fucked Noel's mouth with his tongue as Noel fucked Jai's body with his cock.

Gradually, Jai relaxed beneath Noel's body, lifting his hips to meet Noel's thrusts. His bruising grasp on Noel's hip—which had been cautionary and almost deterring—turned encouraging, pulling Noel in faster. Harder.

Noel knew he'd found Jai's prostate when Jai jolted under him, head falling back on the bed with a shout. Smiling with pride, Noel angled his hips to hit the spot again, and Jai groaned. Jai was expressive during sex, but Noel had never heard these noises from his Other before. They sent pleasure rippling down his spine as sweat gathered in the hollow of Jai's throat.

"Oh fuck. Oh fuck. Oh fuck," Jai chanted, nails sinking into Noel's scarred back.

"I know." Noel pressed their foreheads together as his orgasm built. "I know. But you have to come. Because I—I'm close, and I can't—"

"Come," Jai ordered against Noel's lips, and like an unseen wave smashing into him, Noel's orgasm took him off guard.

His body shuddered and twitched as he was lost to pleasure, and all the while, Jai ran gentle fingers through his hair. He soothed and cooed as Noel came down from the high of ecstasy. Sweet kisses. Tender caresses. Noel preened under the attention.

"You didn't pull out," Jai complained. "Asshole."

Snickering into Jai's shoulder, Noel shook his head. "Sorry."

"I'm just kidding. It's fine."

His body felt heavy as lead, but he forced himself to lift off his Other. Jai watched him with fire roaring in his eyes, and Noel smiled down at him. Jai's cock was still hard, dripping and mixing with the hairs on his stomach. For a moment, Noel felt guilty for coming first, but Jai must have felt it through the bond because he captured Noel's face and kissed him hard.

Before he softened and slipped out of Jai's body, Noel reached between them and stroked Jai's shaft. He offered a few thrusts, his cock over-sensitive, but it was enough. Jai stiffened, then spasmed as he spilled over Noel's fingers. Noel swallowed Jai's moans as his body tightened around Noel's spent cock.

The moment Jai went lax, Noel collapsed on top of him, cum and sweat smearing between them. He slipped out of Jai's ass a moment later, and Jai wrapped his arms around his shoulders and cradled him close as they panted.

"Well," Jai gasped out, "that was... something."

With a snicker, Noel pressed a kiss to his Adam's apple. "Told you you had a prostate."

And Jai threw his head back and laughed.

FRENCH LESSONS

Riley

NOEL'S MAXI DRESS SWAYED around his calves as he twirled and danced through the living room. He sang along with the radio, a sultry French song I didn't know. With every shimmy and turn, his skirt flared around his legs.

It was nice seeing Noel carefree, so I let him dance as I wrapped up the cord of the vacuum and wheeled it into the hallway. Noel was dusting the shelves lined with picture frames as I returned to the living room, and I watched him dance gracefully. He must have felt my gaze because he glanced over his shoulder.

Finding me watching, a sexy grin spread his lips. He added more sway to his hips and crooned at me in French. Under the guise of fluffing the throw pillows, I passed behind him and smacked him on his gyrating butt.

With a laugh, he spun and looped his arms around my neck, yanking me into his body. He continued to dip and weave around me, singing in my ear, and I feigned disinterest as long as I could before I surrendered, allowing him to lead me into a dance. The duster he held tickled the back of my neck as we danced, and I was relieved when he discarded it, the cheap plastic thunking against the carpet somewhere behind me.

Our playful twirls shifted along with the music, and soon, he was pressed tightly to my front, our bodies grinding slow and sensual. I wasn't much of a dancer, especially with my ruined leg, but I held him close, hands trailing down his sides to the hem of his dress.

Slipping a few fingers under the fabric, I traced the skin of his legs. He hummed, dropping the volume of his voice until he was purring the French lyrics. For all I knew, he was singing a spaghetti recipe or something equally not sexy. But the curled words, plus his smooth voice and lithe body flush to mine, sent heat zipping through my veins.

As my body responded, I nuzzled his collarbones on display and brushed aside the thin strap of his dress on his left shoulder. It fell away, dropping low on his biceps, and I kissed the front of his shoulder. My other hand traveled farther north, skating over his thigh.

"We shouldn't get carried away," I said. "Gideon will be home soon."

"I bet we can be stealthy," Noel whispered before capturing my earlobe between his teeth and tugging.

Jai was working a night shift at the infirmary, but Gideon would be home for dinner any minute. This was a terrible idea, and I was about to tell Noel so, but then my fingers met rough fabric—lace—and I groaned. He was wearing panties. I liked it when he wore pretty things.

"Let's go to the bedroom," I said.

He shook his head. "Fuck me right here."

"We'll get caught," I warned, but I knew that was far from a deterrent. Most of the time, Noel liked getting caught. But getting caught by Gideon would not bring the sexy consequences that getting caught by Jai usually brought.

"Riley."

I could hear his pout, and I chuckled. It turned into a moan when he sucked a hickey into the skin of my throat. His erection rubbed against my hip, brushing my own hardness every few minutes, and my resistance quickly diminished.

"If Gideon yells at us for getting cum on the new carpet, I'm blaming you," I grumbled, and Noel withdrew, his colorless eyes glimmering with naughty promises.

"What Gideon doesn't know can't hurt him," he said, leaning his butt against the back of the couch and tilting his head. His hair flowed over his shoulder in an opal wave, and I wanted to sift my fingers through it. Instead, I dropped a hand to my belt and started unbuckling it. His eyes—darkening to violet now—tracked my every move.

"Turn around," I said as I unbuttoned my jeans, and Noel's gaze jumped back to mine.

He bit his bottom lip as color flooded his cheeks and traveled down his neck. "Why?"

My own face heated as I struggled for words. Noel liked dirty talk, but I never felt comfortable with it. Jai was good at finding all the naughty words and making it sound sexy and filthy. But me? I never knew what to say.

Swallowing my reservations, I lowered my zipper and opened my jeans enough to alleviate the pressure on my erection. "Because I told you to," I said, using my firmest voice.

A visible shutter wracked over Noel. "Are you gonna fuck me?"

"I'm going to take care of you," I said, and humor flashed quickly over his features at my inability to curse.

Instead of fighting me further, he made a show of twirling around to present his backside. Slowly, he rested his elbows on the back of the couch and bent over. He craned his neck, watching me over his shoulder with what I could only describe as a sinful smirk on his face.

I closed the distance between us and placed a hand flat on his back between his shoulder blades. I dragged my palm down his spine until I hit his tailbone. I held him there as I gathered the material of his dress in my other hand and hiked it up.

Yellow lace framed the globes of his butt, and I nearly swallowed my tongue. Yellow. My favorite color. God, I loved him so much.

"These for me?" I asked, sneaking a fingertip under the edge of lace.

With a shake of his butt, he said, "Always."

I secured the skirt of his dress around his waist before lowering myself to my knees behind him. My thigh spasmed, but I gritted my teeth against the ache as I curled my fingers into the band of his lacy panties and slowly—*slowly*—drew them down, down, down. They pooled around his ankles, and I left them there.

Guiding his legs apart as far as the panties could stretch, I leaned in and placed a kiss on the back of his right leg, right under his buttcheek. I mimicked the caress on his other leg, molding my palms to his butt. He whimpered as my fingers dug in.

"Riley," he breathed my name like a prayer, and I smiled into his skin.

"Yes?" I spread his cheeks, and goosebumps pebbled over his ivory skin.

"Please."

One word. So simple. But full to the brim with need and desperation.

"I've got you," I reassured him as I trailed kisses up the back of his thighs and over his pale cheeks.

He was pushing back into me before my mouth even made it to my destination. But the moment my lips and tongue touched his wrinkled skin, he moaned, long and loud. I licked languidly, taking my time as he whined and groaned.

Noel loved rimming, both giving and receiving, and he was good at it too. I'd come once from nothing but his tongue inside me, his thumb massaging my taint. And whenever Jai or I prepped him like this, he turned to putty in our hands.

I tongued him until he was soaked with spit, legs trembling, body taut with desire. He was begging, pushing back and riding my mouth as best he could as I held him pinned against the couch. Adding my thumb to the mix, I worked him open until I could press two fingers inside him to massage his prostate with one hand. With my other, I reached around and jerked his hard length.

"Fuck, Riley." Noel panted as his erection leaked over my fingers, slicking the way. "I'm gonna come if you... oh, don't stop. Please, don't stop. Fields of Elysium, your mouth!"

I loved when I pushed him this far, until he was a babbling mess. I wanted to ruin him with pleasure, so I redoubled my efforts, alternating between my fingers and tongue.

"Yes, eat my ass. I wanna come from your tongue." His hand took over on his shaft, so I could focus solely on his request. I ate him out, rubbing a finger over his prostate, as he stroked himself. "Oh, fires of Hell, I'm—shit!"

He stiffened, his channel tightening around my tongue as he came. I prayed he hadn't made a mess of the couch, because I feared it would stain, but as he gasped through his orgasm, I decided I didn't care if it did. I licked and sucked him gently as he came down, massaging the pad of my thumb over his fluttering hole. Once he went slack, I sat back on my heels and caught my breath.

Wiping my mouth, I climbed to my feet, ignoring the stab of pain from my leg. Noel lay slumped over the back of the couch, naked from the waist down, legs spread, completely on display as he panted. The flush of his orgasm was beautiful on his cheek, and a sated smile curled his lips as he remained sprawled for several seconds.

While he recovered, I slid his panties back up his legs and fitted them over his butt. I tucked his softening penis into the lace, wiping away the semen on his tip. Noel barely moved, as I inspected the couch. Crap. Gideon was going to kill us.

My arousal pulsed angrily inside my underwear, annoyed at being ignored this long, but I didn't move to satisfy the need. Noel didn't usually like being topped if he'd already come, so I didn't think he'd want me to finish inside him.

With a contented sigh, Noel straightened, and his dress fell down around him, covering his lacey backside once more. He faced me, his eyes heavy-lidded and satisfied. The spaghetti straps hung on his biceps, lowering his swooping neckline until I could almost see his nipples, and his skin was still a lovely pink color. He was breathtaking.

"You're beautiful," I said, and he beamed at me.

"I want you to come down my throat," he said.

I nearly choked on my own spit. "Oh. Okay."

He chuckled and hauled me close, smothering my mouth with his. We kissed deeply, and I opened for him when his tongue probed at the seam of my lips. I moaned into his mouth, and he swallowed it down as he tackled me—almost roughly—to the carpet.

Pushing my legs apart, he lay down between them, kissing me breathless. His deft fingers shoved at my open jeans until he had the space to slip his hand into my underwear. He removed me from my briefs and stroked me a few times with his dry hand.

Without preamble, he broke the kiss, slithered down my body, and enveloped me, his mouth hot, his tongue wet. My eyes fluttered shut on a groan as my head fell back, hitting the cushioned floor with a dull thunk. Noel's mouth was... heavenly.

I cradled his head tenderly, aware of every move my fingers made through his silky hair. The last thing I wanted was to trigger him, so I kept every touch soft and sweet. His mouth, however, was neither soft nor sweet. He sucked me determinedly, hooking one of my legs over his shoulder as his head bobbed.

Lost to the pleasure, I nearly missed the ripple of shock that sprang through my fiery Committed bond as Noel swallowed around me. My eyes shot open, and I gasped as my gaze met wide green eyes. Gideon stood in the doorway, mouth ajar, knuckles white where his fingers clenched around the doorjamb.

His Adam's apple bobbed, his attention ping-ponging between my face and my groin, where Noel was exuberantly going down on me. I tightened my fingers around the back of Noel's neck, and my fair angel lifted off me. He stiffened, and for a moment, all three of us froze and gaped at each other.

Gideon had witnessed quite a bit in the years we'd been together, but this was the most blatant sexual act he'd interrupted. Though he was never judgmental of my sexual dynamics with Jai and Noel, he wasn't always comfortable being present when things grew intimate. I had a feeling it fed into his own insecurities around *our* physical relationship, but I'd never questioned him. He had limits, and I respected them.

But now? Guilt threatened to choke me as his fingers dug into the trim, jaw tight, throat working. The emotion in his eyes was difficult to discern. There was embarrassment at having stumbled across something private—though we were technically doing this in a public part of the house, so how private had we expected this exchange to remain?—and surprise, of course. I read uncertainty, a twinge of jealousy, and, if I wasn't mistaken, a dash of curiosity. Then Gideon looked away from me and locked gazes with Noel.

Something unsaid passed between them. Noel arched an eyebrow. Gideon audibly swallowed. A dangerous smile broke over Noel's face.

He flicked his starburst eyes to mine and winked. Then he dipped his head and took me back into his mouth.

I made a strangled sound in my throat, opening my mouth to tell him to stop, but I was rendered speechless as Gideon visibly relaxed. His hand fell to his side, and he leaned his shoulder against the doorjamb. His face was still flushed, and he still looked unsure, like he was considering turning tail and bolting. But he didn't.

Cocking his head inquisitively, he offered me a hesitant, almost questioning smile. Like he was double-checking that his presence was welcome. Like he was asking for permission. Like he wanted to stay and... watch.

An unintentional moan slipped from my mouth as Noel circled the head of my penis with his tongue, but the pleasure was equally fueled by Gideon's eyes on me. I'd never been watched like this. Sure, there were times when Jai, Noel, and I were having sex that a pair would be more heavily involved while the third would take a more directorial role or step back to rest or grab supplies. But this, being the sole focus of a voyeur's attention when they had no intention of physically participating, was different.

Gideon didn't speak. He didn't move to join us. He just stood there and watched Noel suck me off like we were starring in a porno.

After all this time, Noel knew exactly how to get me off quickly, but he was clearly playing this up for our audience. He licked and played, offering just enough suction to keep me hard and needy but not enough to push me over the edge. And my God, the sounds he made. He moaned around me, making wet noises as he took me deep, throat spasming.

I was afraid he would scare Gideon off with the exaggerated performance, but Gideon was braver than I gave him credit for sometimes. He didn't run away. He tracked every emotion on my face, drinking in my groans of pleasure. And holy cats, it worked for me.

Apparently, I liked being watched. Heat and desire rushed through me, and I gave myself permission to enjoy every moment of this. I refused to break eye contact with Gideon as I rubbed the back of Noel's neck and moved my hips to the rhythm Noel had established. I moaned and whimpered louder than I might have normally, and Gideon's eyes darkened a shade.

Time held no meaning as I lost myself in the pleasure of Noel's mouth, engulfed in the intensity of Gideon's gaze. And some indeterminable time later, I pushed deep into Noel's throat as I came with a cry. Noel swallowed around me with a moan, and Gideon's eyes glittered as he soaked in the sight of my climax.

As I came down from the high of orgasm, I realized all three of us were breathing hard. Noel rested his forehead on my hip, panting into my jeans. Gideon stared at me in awe, his cheeks ruddy, chest rising and falling in a choppy, labored tempo. And me? I was blissed out.

Noel sat back on his heels, wiping his mouth daintily as he sent Gideon a Cheshire grin. Gideon blushed a deep burgundy color that made me want to kiss his face off. I ran a palm over my face, trying to compose myself.

The silence was awkward, and I looked between Noel and Gideon, waiting for one of them to speak. Noel looked seconds away from bursting into laughter. Gideon rubbed the back of his neck. Then he cleared his throat.

"Pretty dress," he said with a nod to Noel's maxi dress.

Noel blinked in surprise. "Oh. Thanks. It has pockets!" He shoved his hands into said pockets to show them off. Gideon tugged on his ear. I snorted a laugh which I covered with a cough.

Biting his lip to keep from laughing, Noel fixed my jeans as I smiled tentatively up at Gideon. He grinned shyly back, ducking his head. But then his gaze landed on the back of the couch, and the smile turned into a frown.

"You've got to be kidding me," he growled.

Noel and I inspected the stain Noel had left on the fabric with his release, then exchanged a panic look. Then together, we said, "He started it!"

WHAT'S FAMILY FOR?

PART ONE

Noel

JAI SPUN IN LAZY circles in the computer chair that he'd stolen from Martha's office. His head hung over the back of the chair as he stared at the ceiling, spinning, spinning, spinning. He puckered his lips and blew out annoying noises as he not-so-patiently waited.

Doing his best to ignore his Other, Noel focused on his computer screen, filling in reports and adding information to developing adoption cases. Jai started humming under his breath and tapping a rhythm on the arms of the chair, and Noel rolled his eyes.

"I'm working," he sang to mask his irritation.

"And I'm hungry," Jai sang back, somehow managing to slouch deeper into the chair. He was free from work today, and they'd made plans to grab lunch together. But he'd shown up almost an hour too early, and Noel was trying to work around his Other's bored fidgeting.

"You're just going to have to be patient. Go make yourself useful while you wait. Help Nadia with lunchtime."

Like a deer in headlights, Jai froze, eyes wide. "Toddlers bite when they're *not* hungry. If you think I'm going anywhere near them when they are, you're crazy."

Noel laughed openly at that, and Jai scowled. "Of all the things in the universe to be scared of, and you're afraid of babies."

"They bite and spit and shit all over you. And they're too breakable! They have a self-destruct button on the top of their heads for fuck's sake." Jai crossed his arms over his chest like a pouting kid. "I'm not gonna be responsible for squishing one."

Jai's aversion to children was amusing, but there was a secret place inside Noel that ached. Jai was genuinely frightened of babies, and Riley had no desire to be a father. Gideon was content with their lives as it stood now. Which left Noel on an island with his desire for more.

Granted, never being a parent was a small price to pay in exchange for the family he had, but it still stung in the farthest recesses of Noel's heart.

"Children are actually incredibly durable. You're just a pussy."

Jai flipped him off and opened his mouth to retort, but he was interrupted by a knock on Noel's door. They both turned their attention to the door as it opened, and Gideon's face appeared.

"Hey, Gid." Noel set aside his papers as his Prime stepped halfway into the office.

Gideon caught sight of Jai and hesitated. "Is this a bad time?"

He turned to leave, but Jai shook his head as Noel said, "Not at all. Come in."

Hesitating, Gideon straddled the threshold of the office, rubbing the back of his neck. Jai and Noel exchanged a look before Noel said, "Jai and I were going to get lunch soon, so we really aren't busy."

"Right. I forgot that you were free today," Gideon said to Jai.

Jai straightened in his stolen chair. "You wanna come to lunch with us?"

For a moment, it looked like Gideon wanted to turn around and run, and Noel leaned forward and placed his elbows on his desk. "Is everything okay?"

"Is it Riley?" Jai half-stood, but Gideon was already shaking his head.

"No, everything's fine. Riley's in class as far as I know." The large Archangel shut the door firmly behind him, then stuck his hands into the pockets of his slacks. He shifted his weight awkwardly, avoiding eye contact. "I just wanted to talk to Noel about something, but I can come back."

A muscle ticked in Jai's jaw, and Noel thought he saw hurt flit over his features. "Oh. I can leave you two if..."

"No," Gideon said too quickly. "It's... fine."

Noel's curiosity was piqued, and he sat back in his chair, folding his hands over his stomach. He gestured to the chair on the other side of his desk. "Do you want to sit down?"

Judging from his expression, Gideon really didn't want to sit down, but he did anyway. "Okay." He hastily took a seat, lifting his right foot and resting his ankle on his left knee. His fingers drummed on his shin as he observed Noel's messy desk, then studied Jai's wary posture.

Noel watched the blond man fidget in concerned confusion. Gideon leaned back in his chair, lowering his right leg until both feet were flat on the floor. He twined his fingers over his stomach. Then he sat forward, propping his elbows on his knees. The longer he sat, the more flustered he grew until his cheeks were pink.

Once again, Jai and Noel exchanged a look of confusion.

"You, uh, doing okay there, Gid?" Jai asked.

"Yes. Of course. Why wouldn't I be?"

Gideon's nonchalance rang false, and Noel tried not to laugh as he said, "I don't know. You just look like you're about to get a colonoscopy without anesthesia."

With a grimace, Gideon tugged on his ear, then scrubbed a palm down his face. "I need help with something."

Noel propped his elbows on the arms of his chair and rested his chin on the back of his laced fingers. "Okay."

"It's"—Gideon shot Jai a guarded look as his cheeks flushed darker—"delicate."

Jai cocked an offended eyebrow. "Don't give me that look. I can be delicate as shit."

Noel bit his bottom lip to stave off a smile and failed.

"Right," Gideon said, clearly disagreeing as he glared at the floor. "It's just... I'm, uh... it's embarrassing."

Before Jai could speak and scare Gideon off for good, Noel rose and rounded his desk, stopping in front of Gideon. He leaned his ass against the desk and crossed his ankles. The tip of his boot brushed Gideon's loafers. "Is something wrong?"

Gideon shook his head, crossing his arms over his chest. "It's about Riley's birthday coming up."

When he hesitated, Jai grunted impatiently. "And?"

Noel shot his Other a look to shut him up, and Jai sat back in his chair with his hands raised in surrender. He mimed zipping his lips shut, and Noel rolled his eyes before returning his attention to Gideon.

"And," he prompted gently.

Gideon grimaced. "I wanted to get something for him, but I don't know which one—I've never had to buy one before. And there's just so many of them to choose from, and I'm not sure which ones are better suited for Riley's... needs." He buried his flushed face in his hands. "I know you—well, both of you—have... experience with these kinds of things. I thought—you know what? It's stupid. Never mind."

Nearly tripping over himself, Gideon stood abruptly and tried to flee. Noel chased him down and cut off his escape as Jai jumped to his feet, sending his chair skittering across the floor. There was no way either of them were letting Gideon leave without getting to the bottom of his embarrassment. Placing a hand on his defined chest, Noel smiled kindly up at him, palm rubbing soothing circles.

"Gideon, calm down. You know you can talk to us about anything." He patted that impressive pectoral muscle. "But I'm not quite tracking with you. So what is it that you're looking for?"

Sighing in defeat, Gideon hung his head, as if in shame, as he mumbled a quiet, "A vibrator."

Jai made a choking sound somewhere behind Noel, and he himself had to swallow a noise of shocked amusement as he coughed and sputtered. "Oh. Well, that's... okay."

With a groan, Gideon side-stepped out of Noel's reach and hid his face in his hands again. "This is humiliating."

"No, it's not," Noel said as Jai snorted out, "Gid, come on. We've been together how long now? We don't really have secrets from each other anymore."

"Yeah," Noel agreed. "For Trinity's sake, you watched me suck Riley off that one time, remember?"

"What?" Jai demanded, hands falling on his hips with a frown. "Why wasn't I invited?"

Ignoring Jai, Gideon paled white as a sheet and pointed an accusing finger at Noel. "That was an accident!"

"You walking in on it was an accident," Noel said with a teasing grin. "But I feel like the staying and the watching was less of an accident and more of a choice."

"Oh, come on!" Jai threw his hands up. "How am I only now finding out about this? You guys suck."

Face red as a brick house, Gideon stammered unintelligibly for far too long before Noel took pity on the poor man. "Gideon, it's okay. It was hot, and Riley loved it. We don't have to be weird about it," he said, though he shot Jai a meaningful look. "It's just sex."

Jai looked like he'd swallowed a lemon, but he gritted out a begrudging, "Yeah, it's just sex."

"Maker, strike me down," Gideon lamented in a show of uncharacteristic dramatics. "Set me to sail and bring me to Elysium."

"Wow, I never thought I'd accuse you of being a drama queen." Jai laughed into his hand, though he tried to cover it with a cough, and Gideon glowered at him.

Noel hooked his thumbs into the belt loops of his skinny jeans and chuckled lightly. "Stop it, both of you. You're being ridiculous." He checked the time on his phone. "I know a good shop here in Utopia, and it's time for a lunch break. We can go—"

Gideon balked. "Now?"

"You really want to draw this out?" Jai asked.

"I have a few ideas of what Riley might like. Jai might too. I know..." Noel tread cautiously, quirking his head questioningly at Jai. "You two use toys, right?"

A dangerous grin curled Jai's lips. "I don't think Gideon's looking for the kind of toys Riley and I use."

Well, now Noel was curious, but he was also slightly frightened of the glint in Jai's eye. "Okay, well, Riley and I play around with pretty tame stuff, so..."

"Depths of Sheol," Gideon muttered. "Fine. Let's get this over with."

Without waiting for another word, Gideon yanked the door open and practically fled the office. Noel and Jai smirked at each other, silently laughing at their flustered Prime.

"This is gonna be fucking fun," Jai said, and Noel couldn't help but agree.

WHAT'S FAMILY FOR?

PART TWO

Jai

THE WALK TO THE sex shop was awkwardly devoid of conversation, but Jai was almost giddy with excitement anyway. He whistled a happy tune as Noel walked quietly beside Gideon. Gideon, who was wound tighter than a two dollar watch. Jai wanted to tease him, but he held back.

If Gideon's embarrassment was born from the general awkwardness that the topic of sex could bring to a conversation, Jai would have flayed him alive with innuendos and mortifying questions. But he wasn't a complete and total asshole. At least, not all the time.

Humiliating Gideon about his and Riley's sex life would be incredibly detrimental. Jai might not have known all the details surrounding his Committed's physical relationship with his Prime, but he knew Gideon, and some insecurities lingered forever. There might always be a part of Gideon that would never feel adequate in regard to his sexual dynamic with Riley, and Jai would rather carve out his own tongue than feed that particular monkey on Gideon's back.

Riley's love and acceptance had gone a long way in building Gideon's self-worth, but in the end, the only person who could truly change Gideon's perception of himself was Gideon. But offering support was never a bad thing, right?

Never in his near three hundred years of life had Jai thought he'd be accompanying Gideon and Noel to a sex shop to purchase a vibrator for the Committed they shared. Life was fucking weird, that was for damn sure.

Upon arrival at the store, Gideon hesitated, eyeing the door handle like it would sprout fangs and attack. Noel sighed, grabbing the handle and tugging the door open. Waving Gideon inside, he muttered under his breath about unhealthy sex shame, and Jai bit his tongue to keep from laughing.

Like Gideon was trying to make himself smaller—or maybe invisible?—he hunched down and stared at the floor as they walked into the shop. The bell chimed overhead, announcing their presence, and Gideon flinched.

"Well, hey, Grace. Ophelia," Noel greeted the two women who were in the middle of paying for their purchase—a purple dildo so large it had Jai wincing in sympathy. Sure, he let Noel and Riley top him every once in a while, but Hades, there was no way in this realm or any other that he'd let something that big near his ass.

Gideon's face turned a frightening shade of puce as the former councilwoman turned and smiled at them. "Noel. Jai. Gideon? Fancy seeing you here."

Unable to resist the temptation to tease Gideon, just a little, Jai knocked his elbow against Gideon's obnoxiously. "Oh, you know, gotta keep the spark alive, right?"

The women laughed as Noel covered his smile with his palm. Ophelia, Grace's Fallen Committed, tucked the impressive phallus into a bag and faced them as Gideon did his best to melt into the floor. Gideon glared at Jai. Jai smiled sweetly back at him.

"We'll leave you to it," Ophelia said, slipping her hand into Grace's and giving a tug. "Come on, love."

Hands clasped, the women breezed past them, and Noel waved brightly. Gideon bowed slightly, muttering an unintelligible farewell. Jai opened the door for them, bidding them farewell. They giggled between themselves like lovestruck teenagers as the door shut behind them.

"I want to die," Gideon said mournfully.

"Get over it," Noel said with a playful shove to Gideon's shoulder.

"Come on!" Jai snapped his fingers and marched toward the back wall. "Let's find Riley a prostate vibrator."

"Say it louder, why don't you?" Gideon snarled.

Noel tried to appease him. "There's no one else here."

As Noel and Jai browsed, Gideon eyed the contents of the store with a complicated expression on his face. He looked equal parts curious, scared, and embarrassed. He poked at a neon green silicone horse dildo, then picked up a Dirk Yates AM 80 Ass Missile. His green eyes were wide as he brandished it at Noel.

"Is this..."

Noel grinned and winked. "Anything's a dildo if you're brave enough."

"Maker have mercy." Gideon set the prostate missile aside as if it was actually a weapon of mass destruction.

"Weapon of *ass* destruction." Jai poked Noel's arm. "Get it? 'Cause it's a missile."

Noel burst into laughter as Gideon stared at them both with a pained expression on his face. "Sometimes, I feel like the only adult," he grumbled.

"Do you buy vibrators for all your children?" Jai asked flippantly as he read the packaging label of a cockcage.

He didn't see or hear Gideon move, and he yelped when Gideon's hand landed on the back of his head. It hurt, and Jai stumbled out of reach, rubbing his head.

"What the fuck, Gid? I'm kidding."

"Stop teasing him," Noel admonished softly before rubbing Gideon's arm. "We're just playing around. Come on, we gotta cut the awkwardness somehow."

Gideon tugged on his ear, face aflame. "This isn't easy for me," he admitted, and Jai placed the cockcage back on the shelf.

"I know. Sorry. You know I'd never seriously fuck with you about this, right? I'm just giving you the same shit I'd give Noel."

At that, Gideon almost smiled. "Yeah, I know. I'm being too sensitive about this, aren't I?"

Noel pinched his forefinger and thumb together. "Just a teensy bit."

"All right, all right." Gideon backed down. "Sorry. Make all the sex jokes you want."

"Oh Maker, don't give Jai that kind of freedom!" Noel screeched as a flash of yellow caught Jai's eye.

He chortled to himself as he plucked the package containing the prostate massager from the wall. "Eureka!"

"Is that a good one?" Gideon asked hesitantly.

"It's yellow." Jai tossed it to Noel, who read the packing.

"It's flexible, easy to keep clean, and"—Noel waggled his eyebrows—"remote controlled."

Something flashed in Gideon's green eyes, and he took the vibrator from Noel to inspect it. "Oh, well, that would be… more than acceptable."

Jai left them to analyze the toy and plucked a string of anal beads from the wall. He and Riley had never used them, and he contemplated purchasing them. He wasn't sure if Riley would be into it, but Riley was growing more and more adventurous. The longer they were together, the more free Riley felt to explore and try new things, especially in the bedroom.

Sure, he had hard limits—everyone did. Jai couldn't tie him up with anything inanimate because it triggered memories of being trapped in a hospital bed or secured in Leviathan's lab chair. And any type of blindfold was iffy. Riley had tried it once or twice, but he had to be in the right headspace for it, otherwise, he would freak out.

But that was okay. There were lots of ways Jai could dominate him that satisfied both their needs.

Jai tuned back into Gideon and Noel's conversation as Noel said, "I suggest getting him this and see how you both like it. Until you try a few different kinds, you won't know for sure what your preferences are, but this is a great place to start."

"Do you—" Gideon cut off his own question with a choked sound. "Never mind. That's none of my—"

"Yes," Noel answered him, unashamed. "Riley and I play with toys, and I am confident he will like this one."

Yeah, Riley would definitely like it. Jai knew because he had a similar one tucked away in his side table that he and Riley used quite often. He'd pin Riley down and slowly speed up the vibration, edging his Committed until Riley would plead for release. It was a sweet torture that sent Riley out of his mind, and Maker help him, Jai liked it when Riley begged.

He blinked away the memories before he chubbed up in his jeans, watching Gideon read the back of the packaging as he chewed on the inside of his cheek. "And it won't..." He drifted off, but Jai and Noel remained quiet, offering him time to gather his thoughts. "I won't hurt him with this, right?"

Well, damn. How it was possible for someone as big and badass as Gideon to be adorable, Jai would never know. But fuck, it was cute how deeply Gideon cared. Noel must have agreed because he currently had a sappy smile on his face.

"As long as you and Riley communicate while using it, it won't hurt him," Noel said.

"I don't think we need to tell you this, but Riley knows his own body, and he'll tell you if something isn't working," Jai added. Gideon didn't look convinced, and Jai cleared his throat, feeling truly awkward for the first time as he said, "He's called red before. With me. If he isn't into it, he'll tell you."

Both Noel and Gideon blushed at Jai's admission, but neither of them commented. They were all aware, to a certain extent, the dynamics Riley had with each of them, but they never disclosed personal details. Riley's relationships with each of them were private, and it was a limit they respected with each other, as well as with Riley.

"You're right," Gideon said quietly. "Riley and I don't... you're right. It'll be fine."

With a simper, Noel rubbed Gideon's back, propping his head on Gideon's shoulder. "For what it's worth, I think it's very sweet of you."

"Seeking your help to purchase a sex toy because I am entirely inept doing it myself?" Gideon deadpanned.

"Self pity doesn't become you, Gideon," Noel chided lightly.

"Yeah," Jai slapped Gideon on the shoulder. "Now come on. Let's buy it before you get cold feet."

"Thank you," Gideon whispered as they exited the shop five minutes later. "Both of you. I... thanks."

Noel rose onto his toes and smacked a wet kiss to Gideon's cheek. "Of course. What is family for?"

"Buying sex toys together, apparently," Jai said, and Gideon finally cracked a full smile. He even chuckled, and Noel beamed at them both. And Jai found himself smiling too. His family was fucking weird, but it was the best thing he had, and he wasn't giving it up. Not ever.

WINTER SOLSTICE

PART ONE

Riley

THE STARS TWINKLED OVERHEAD as jovial music filtered through the air. Fairy lights sparkled in the trees lining the main road. Businesses had opened their doors, spilling their patrons into the street. Food and drink circulated through the crowd, and the atmosphere was joyous and loose—a little too loose thanks to the flowing ambrosia.

It was a warm night, but all nights in Elysium were warm. Thankfully, my yellow shirt was light and airy, sheer in the front to show off skin and the subtlest of muscle definition.

The leather leggings Noel had insisted upon stuck to my legs like a second skin, but the discomfort was worth the boost in confidence they instilled. Jai hadn't been able to take his eyes off me since we'd left the house, and I knew it was only a matter of time until he whisked me away to some dark corner to satisfy the simmering want thrumming through our bond.

Searching the crowd, I sipped my wine and smiled in greeting to a few acquaintances. I spotted Noel across the road talking with Grace and her Fallen Committed, Ophelia. Ophelia bounced a baby on her hip as Grace laughed at something she said. Noel cooed at the baby, smile wide as tiny hands grabbed at his long, pearly hair.

My heart twisted at the sight. Noel was a natural with kids, and he loved babies. In quiet moments late at night, he'd whisper his most secret dreams into my chest, and I would always promise to find a way to bring them to fruition. All except this. I didn't think I was strong enough to give him this particular desire.

Kids were... terrifying. Sure, I worked with students but never before they were ten years old. And it was only a few hours, not enough time for me to truly screw them up. But kids? In our house? In our family? Every parental figure during my formative years had either died, abandoned me, abused me, or neglected me. It didn't set the best precedent.

Plus, I wasn't the only one averse to children. Jai was legitimately scared of them. He would never admit it of course, but there was a reason he did his best to avoid visiting Noel when he was at work. The first time we'd stopped by to see Noel's office, a baby had crawled over to play with Jai's shiny boot buckles, and my fierce angel had cowered against the wall, freezing like a statue.

"It's touching me," he'd hissed, eyes wide and panicked. "What do I do?"

"Um, pick him up?" Noel had said with a confused frown, and Jai blanched.

"I'm not touching that thing. They bite—eep!" And Jai made the strangest whimpering sound as the toddler attempted to climb up his leg. "It's attacking! Riley, help me."

None of us had helped him. Actually, we'd laughed. A lot. It may have been cruel, but I'd never seen Jai afraid of anything the way he feared babies. Maker help me, it was hilarious.

Humor aside, I didn't see how we could bring kids into our family without giving Jai an aneurysm. Gideon, on the other hand, had no problems with kids. He always smiled kindly and hunkered down to be as small as possible so as not to scare them away. It must have worked because children loved him. Using Gideon as a jungle gym was their favorite pastime anytime Gideon helped Noel at the adoption center.

But as much as Gideon enjoyed playing with the children, I didn't know how he'd feel about upsetting our familial dynamic by adding kids to the mix. I loved how things were now, just the four of us. We had freedom to do whatever we wanted whenever we wanted to do it. Having kids would take that freedom from us, and I feared Noel was the only one willing to make that sacrifice.

We had time, of course. There was no rush. But seeing Noel light up as he cuddled Grace and Ophelia's daughter to his chest made me ache. He never wore that expression at home. It was always reserved for the children he fought so hard for every day.

"I know that look," a voice rasped in my ear as the scent of *dokha* swirled around me.

I smiled into my wine glass. "What look?"

Jai's arms wrapped around me from behind, nose skimming the shell of my ear. "The *I-want-to-give-Noel-whatever-he-wants* look."

"It's hard to resist when he looks that happy," I said, and Jai sighed.

"The list of why kids are a bad idea for us is a mile long, Riles."

"I know," I said. "It's just... he wants that kind of future for us, and it feels selfish to withhold it from him."

"I know, baby. But it's not something we can consider lightly." He nuzzled the tattooed skin behind my ear, pressing his lips to the place I knew the *J* to be.

I finally found the guts to get the tattoo last year. I'd wanted it for a long time, but I wasn't one to seek out pain voluntarily. I had enough pain in my daily life from my bum leg and the trauma of my past; I didn't need any extra.

But when Noel had finished the design—a near perfect replica of the tattoo Alter Riley had on his neck—I couldn't wait another day. Noel rented a booth in an Utopian tattoo shop and permanently marked my neck. Vines cascaded from behind my ear to my back, ending at the first notch of my spine. Within the ivy were the letters *J*, *N*, and *G*; yet another symbol of my love and devotion.

For them, our bonds were enough. They didn't need rings, even though they'd gifted me one on my thirty-fifth birthday. And they didn't need tattoos. Well, Jai had tattoos, but that was more because he loved the sensation of needles in his skin. Masochist.

To cover the scar puckering the skin above his heart where he'd taken Asmodeus's dagger, Jai had asked Noel to design a tattoo using the Utopian symbol for eternity and both Noel's and my names. It was a beautiful tattoo, the black ink gorgeous against Jai's olive skin.

I loved putting my palm there when I rode him, my name tattooed into his skin as his hard length stretched me to the breaking point.

Blinking back to the present, I turned in Jai's hold and wrapped one arm around his neck as I held my wine to my chest. His dark eyes smoldered, the fire behind his irises flickering, and I lifted my face in a silent request for a kiss. He obliged with a chuckle, his lips sliding over mine as his beard bit into my chin.

"I don't want to talk about depressing things," I mumbled into the kiss. "Tonight's the winter solstice. We're here to have fun."

When his hands molded over my butt, he waggled his eyebrows mischievously. "I can think of many ways we can have fun."

"And they're all appropriate for the public, I'm sure," I drawled, and he grinned.

"Well, I don't know about that." His long fingers squeezed me, and our bond flared.

He was hard against my belly, and I melted into him as he kissed me, his tongue slipping into my mouth and tangling with mine. His piercing was warm, and I shivered at the memory of it massaging my most secret skin. Both Jai and Noel were extremely proficient lovers, but I had a weakness for that tongue piercing.

"Come with me," he purred, and I found myself nodding.

Dragging me away from the crowd, Jai handed my wine off to a random angel, and I blushed as the stranger gave us a knowing grin. I limped after Jai, my hand clasped tightly in his. Apparently, I wasn't gimping along fast enough, so he swept me into his arms and carried me into a dark alley.

Music and voices from the festival drifted from the mouth of the alley, and I protested as Jai set me down. "Someone will see," I hissed, and he chuckled darkly.

"That's half the fun, shortstack."

"Just because you're an exhibitionist—"

He didn't let me finish. Spinning me around, he pressed me face-first into the brick wall. He rolled his hips against my butt, his erection hot and hard. As he ground himself against me, he snaked a hand around my hip and rubbed at the front of my leather leggings. I hardened for him, moaning into the brick.

"Jai, we're gonna... get caught... oh my God." I shuddered as his hand dove under my waistband and circled my shaft. My leggings were too tight to offer much room for movement, but as his thumb circled the head, pleasure zipped down my spine.

"Where's your sense of adventure?" He sucked on my neck, and I laughed. "Is this okay?"

His movements halted, his voice losing the teasing note. If I said no, if I told him I didn't want to continue so close to the festival, he would stop, no questions asked. While he enjoyed pushing my boundaries and comfort zone, he never took anything I wasn't willing to give. Consent was a very important aspect for all four of us.

"Yes," I confessed into the brick, simultaneously ashamed and turned on at the thought of having sex within ear shot of practical strangers. "I'm good. Just... don't let anyone see me."

I heard the smile in his voice as he worked to open the buttons of my leather pants. "It's too dark. If you're loud, they might hear. But if they try to look, they won't be able to see who we are." He bit my earlobe gently. "They'll just know a pretty little twink is getting fucked good and hard."

"Oh God." I was a sucker for his dirty talk.

"Do you want that, baby?" he crooned as he slid leather over my hips, exposing my skin to the night air. "Do you want to be my pretty little twink?"

My face burned in embarrassment even as I nodded pathetically. "Yes, Jai."

"Good boy." As my leggings pooled around my ankles, Jai groaned. "You're not wearing underwear."

"The leather was tight," I said.

"Oh, I know. That tight leather has been driving me crazy all night." A plastic packet tore moments before two slick fingers pushed between my cheeks. "Ass out, Riley." I obeyed, and he kissed my cheek. "Such a good boy."

Propping my forearms on the brick, I rested my forehead on my arms and closed my eyes. I lost myself to the feel of his fingers stretching me, the heat of him at my back, the rough calluses in his palm as he stroked me in time with every thrust of his fingers. He played me like one of his instruments, and I surrendered.

Before I knew it, he was pushing into me, the head of his erection stretching the first ring of muscles. I relaxed and bore down. He entered me in one long, slow thrust, and I mewled in pleasure.

"So good," he said. "You feel so good, baby."

"Don't stop," I begged. "Jai, please, I need…"

"I'm gonna give you what you need."

With a tug on my curls, he yanked my head to the side and smashed our mouths together in a filthy kiss. I whimpered as he canted his hips, his frenum piercing massaging my prostate with every undulation.

I met his thrusts, my breath puffing out of me in harsh bursts. His fingers in my hair tightened, and my scalp prickled as he hauled me upright, my back to his chest, my palms on the brick. With one hand around my throat, he directed my head to the side.

"Say Noel's name when you come," he commanded, and my eyes met dark purple ones lined in charcoal.

Noel smiled, a wicked curve to his full lips as he rubbed the heel of his hand over the bulge in his light skinny jeans. His tank top was flowy and colorful, longer in the back than in the front. His eyelids were dusted with reds, yellows, and oranges. He was so beautiful.

"Noel," I gasped out his name as my orgasm tingled in my belly. Then lower where Jai pegged my prostate in a fast, hard rhythm. The bonds burned, and I… "Noel-Noel-Noel."

As my orgasm rolled through me, Jai slowed his tempo, his length sliding in and out of me almost lazily. My release splattered the brick wall, and I realized I'd come without touching my erection. That didn't always happen, but I enjoyed every second of it.

When I finally came down from the high, Jai was still rock hard inside me. I waited for him to resume so he could finish, but he pulled out gently with a kiss to my sweaty temple.

"You did so good, baby. You were perfect," he praised as he knelt and tugged my leather pants back up my legs. He wiped the last remnants of cum from my softening penis with his thumb, then licked it away before fastening my pants.

"But you didn't come," I said as I turned around, my chest still heaving.

His dark jeans sagged on his hips, his erection standing long and proud. He'd tucked the band of his boxers underneath his balls, but that was the extent he'd undressed. For some reason, that was sexier than if he'd stripped.

"I still plan to," he said with an evil grin. Then he turned his attention to Noel. "Come here, No."

Swinging his hips, Noel sauntered toward us. His heels clicked with every step he took, his shirt billowing from the breeze. He'd worn his hair down tonight, the strands glimmering in the moonlight.

"I thought you two were up to no good," he said with a wind chime laugh. "Fucking in the alley. Tsk, tsk."

"I'm gonna fuck you in the alley," Jai said, and Noel laughed harder.

"You're assuming I put out."

"Noel." It was just a name, but with the way it rumbled from Jai's chest and off his tongue, it sounded like something scandalous and wonderful. "You're gonna put out."

Noel was close enough to touch, but Jai didn't reach for him. Not yet. Jai tilted his chin, having to look up to meet his Other's gaze since Noel was in heels. Fingers already unbuttoning his jeans, Noel simpered.

"I suppose if you make it good," he challenged. "Then I'll let you fuck me in this alley."

And Jai sent him the smuggest smirk. "I always make it good."

With a wink in my direction, Noel said, "Promise, promises."

Like he'd done with me, Jai trapped Noel against the wall, and I watched with rapt attention as he finished opening Noel's jeans. "Holy shit," he groaned. "Noel, are you wearing panties?"

Noel's gleeful cackle was answer enough, and my penis gave a valiant twitch in my pants at the thought.

"I love it when you wear panties," Jai confessed, mirroring my own thoughts.

"I know you do," Noel said, cocky as a peacock. "Are you gonna make me come in my silk panties, Jairus?"

"You bet your sweet ass I am," he growled against Noel's neck. "And you're gonna keep the heels on."

My fair angel tilted his face to the night sky and laughed.

WINTER SOLSTICE

PART TWO

Riley

BY THE TIME WE'D made ourselves presentable, Noel had yet to banish the flush of arousal from his cheeks. I had the bitter aftertaste of cum on the back of my tongue, and Jai was grinning like the cat that caught the canary.

People would probably know what we'd been up to when we walked out of the alley, but I wasn't going to be ashamed of our love. Plus, no one would guess the secrets we were taking with us, like Noel's soiled, silk panties tucked away in

Jai's back pocket or the small plug in Noel's hole, keeping Jai's release from leaking out and soaking through his skinny jeans.

Leaning on Noel a little more than usual, I tried to walk the stiffness out of my leg. Crouching to suck Noel while Jai took him from behind had been a poor decision, and my thigh was not happy. But Noel didn't complain; he simply shouldered more of my weight to alleviate the pressure on my ruined muscle.

"We can go home if you—" Jai started, but I interrupted him.

"I'm fine. Just gotta push through it." I popped onto my toes and kissed him, then did the same to Noel. "Thank you for joining us."

Noel chuckled against my mouth. "It was my pleasure."

I kissed him thoroughly, fingers sifting through his soft hair, inhaling his lilac scent. "I love you," I said when we parted, and he beamed at me.

"I love you too."

"What am I? Chopped liver?" Jai groused, and both Noel and I rolled our eyes.

"We love you too," we said at the same time, and Jai flicked my ear and poked Noel's side.

"Sure, sure."

There was a raucous off to the side, and I heard a familiar belligerent voice. My heart dropped to my toes as Uriel stumbled through the crowd, a lopsided scowl on his face. The burns from the grenade that took Obie's life hadn't changed a bit in the decades since the battle. Uriel's flesh on the left side of his face was warped and red from his temple to his collar, descending further beneath his clothes.

How he hadn't lost anything vital was a miracle. His left eye had survived, though the vision was marginally poorer than the right. He hadn't lost the use of his hand; the digits were often stiff and sore, but he could still use them. Since I spent a lot of time showering puke and alcohol off of him, I knew the scars covered almost the entire left side of his body, stopping a few inches above his knee.

As usual, Uriel was intoxicated. It was a near constant state of being for him nowadays. Not that there was anything wrong with enjoying ambrosia sometimes, but he did it out of necessity because being sober hurt too much, and he couldn't face the pain.

The worst part of his drinking was that it made him so damn mean.

"Fuck you," Uriel was snarling at anyone and everyone. "Wasn't doing anything. Can't a guy just walk around a festival? Bloody crucifixion."

He drifted off when his sea-green eyes met mine. "Great," he grumbled. "Fucking perfect. Gonna yell at me too? Huh?"

"Hi, Uriel. How are you? It's good to see you. It's been a while." I crossed my arms over my chest. "Those are only a few of the appropriate greetings you can use to address friends who love and care about you."

"Har, har, har," he mocked. "Were you always this annoying? Holy Trinity." He ran a scarred hand through his brown hair, making it stick up in a thousand different directions. "I'm outta here."

He turned to go as a group of young kids stumbled past. I recognized Jesse's messy mop of golden hair moments before someone—Kelly, I realized—pushed Jesse in jest. Given that Jesse wasn't the most coordinated of people, it was no surprise that he tripped and crashed. Right into Uriel.

Jesse's beer soaked the front of Uriel's shirt, and his laughter choked off into a terrified squeak. "Oh shit, I'm so sorry!"

"Watch where the fuck you're going!" Uriel roared, and Jesse cowered with a whimper, golden eyes wide with fear.

"I'm sorry, sir. It was an accident," he said, and Uriel's furious glare cooled slightly.

Wiping beer from his neck and face, my mentor flicked the excess liquid at Jesse. The poor kid flinched.

"Uriel," I said, tugging on his elbow. "He didn't mean to. It was an accident." To Jesse, I said, "Be more careful next time."

"Yes, Master Riley," he said even though he was twenty years old and wasn't my student anymore.

"I know you, don't I?" Uriel waggled his scarred finger in Jesse's face. "Yeah, yeah, I know you. I rage-fucked your mouth once, didn't I?"

Jesse paled white as a sheet before his cheeks and neck splotched red with humiliation. "Uh..."

"Oh my God, Uriel!" I smacked my idiot mentor's shoulder as hard as I could, and he yelped.

Turning his glower on me, he punched me in the sternum with his scarred hand, and we both said, "Ow!"

"Just leave me alone!" He cradled his burnt hand to his chest, shooting Jesse another indecipherable look. "The next time your throat needs a workout, boy, you know where to find me," he said in a sexy croon.

And Jesse said, "Eep! Yes, sir."

As Uriel stomped away, I stared at Jesse, and Jesse stared back, looking like a younger, more innocent version of his sire. I'd known him since he was an infant. I'd taught him; I'd trained him. And now, I knew way too much about his sex life. And how his sex life converged with Uriel's—oh my God!

"We never speak of this again?" I suggested, and Jesse bobbed his head up and down so hard I feared it would roll right off his neck.

"Yes, please," he said, voice strangled.

Fighting laughter, Kelly grabbed Jesse's arm and dragged him away. "Bye, Master Riley," Kelly called as Jesse buried his flushed face in his hands.

"By, Kel." I raked a hand through my curls and sighed. "I really wish I hadn't witnessed that."

"They're not kids anymore. Don't be a prude," Jai said.

Noel grimaced. "Yeah, but Uriel is not in a healthy place. And Jesse's so young."

"It's none of our business," I said quickly, even as worry ate at my gut. I might have to talk to Jesse... or Uriel. Either conversation would be equally terrible.

With a kiss to my scalp, Jai took my hand and squeezed it. "Worries for another day. We're at a party, remember? Tonight, we're having fun."

"Ooh, let's go find Gideon, and see if he's beaten Gabriel's ass at poker yet." Noel took my other hand. "Gideon always drinks too much when they play, and Gabriel's a sore loser. It's always entertaining."

"Not if they start throwing fists," I grumbled.

"They haven't gotten into a drunken brawl in, like, a decade," Noel said dismissively.

Navigating through the partying Utopians, we found the group of tables sectioned off for different casino games. A large group was gathered around one particular table, and I released Jai and Noel's hands and shoved through the crowd.

Gabriel was complaining—no surprise there—and Michael and Gideon were laughing. When I finally pushed past the edge of the circle, I almost smashed into Gabriel's chair.

As if he sensed my proximity, Gabriel glanced over his shoulder, a glare already in place. I smiled serenely at him, and his glare darkened to a glower.

"Hybrid," he sniffed.

"Gabriel," I greet cordially before circling the table to Gideon's side.

My Committed greeted me with a huge smile and an unexpected kiss. I *oomphed* into his mouth as he yanked me onto his lap. He tasted like mint and ambrosia. Ah, that explained it. Gideon was a surprising light-weight. Even a few goblets of ambrosia-infused wine was enough to lower his inhibitions.

"Hi," I said the moment he disconnected our mouths.

"Hello, darling. I'm so glad you're here." He waved his hand over the pile of poker chips in front of him with a flourish. "Look! I'm winning."

"Well done." I wiggled until I was seated more comfortably on his lap, my legs hanging over his thigh as his arm wrapped around my back for support. "You've always been a good poker player."

His green eyes sparkled, his stare slightly glassy from ambrosia. "And now my good luck charm is here. These suckers don't stand a chance."

Gabriel's lips pinched, but Michael just snorted. "You, dear brother, are drunk."

"Only a little," Gideon admitted to me in a whisper. To Michael, he said with over-the-top bravado, "And yet I'm still beating your sober ass."

"Are we going to play?" Gabriel sipped his wine. "Or are you going to be too distracted by your little tart there?"

With a cock of my head, I turned to Gideon. "How is that an insult? Tarts are delicious."

"If you were a tart, you would be the most delectable tart in all the realms," Gideon said seriously, and I preened.

"Thanks, Giddy."

Tossing a chip into the center pile, Gideon glared at Gabriel. "I raise."

"Call."

Michael's dark eyes darted between his brothers before he slapped his cards onto the table. "I fold."

Gabriel grinned triumphantly. "Well, I have a flush." He laid down his cards showing his flush of spades. "Read them and weep."

"Pity," Gideon lamented as he splayed his cards on the table. "Pity for you, I mean, since I have a full house."

The crowd *oohed* and *ahhed* as Gabriel snarled in defeat. I helped Gideon rake in his chips, and Michael laughed as Gabriel grumpily rose from the table.

"Don't forget," Michael called after Gabriel, and the Archangel paused in his retreat to listen. "Martha is expecting you all for dinner next week."

"We'd be delighted," I said as Gideon's hand at my waist squeezed in satisfaction.

We looked at Gabriel. He did not seem delighted, but his grouchy mask slipped slightly as he nodded. "I wouldn't want to disappoint Martha."

"You can bring a tart of your own, if you like," Michael said, and Gabriel flushed to the tips of his ears.

"I don't... there will be no tart," he said between clenched teeth before he spun in a swirl of robes and disappeared into the crowd.

"Well, he was in a good mood tonight," Gideon said cheerfully.

Good mood? How drunk was he?

After cashing in his chips—the funds going toward the Utopian school system—Gideon led me toward the center of the street designated for dancing. The music was happy but slow, and I eyed him warily as he pulled me close.

"I can't dance," I said, gesturing to my leg.

"Just trust me." He squeezed my hand as his arm wrapped around my back. Straightening to his full height, he supported almost my entire weight on his arm, leaving my feet barely touching the ground at all.

Shaking my head, I relaxed into him and allowed him to turn us in a leisurely circle. "Aren't you just a problem solver."

"It's one of my many talents," he joked.

"As is humility," I said, and he chortled.

As Gideon held me close, we swayed to the music. Jai and Noel danced nearby, arguing over who was leading until Jai finally gave in. He allowed Noel to twirl him around the street. They were smiling and laughing, stars in their eyes.

Our bonds were calm and soothing and warm.

"How good are my chances of having you to myself tonight?" Gideon asked, his lips whispering over my brow.

"I'd say they're pretty good." I kissed his jaw, twisting my fingers in his dark blond waves. "Though you're drunk, so no hanky-panky," I teased.

"How will I ever survive," he drawled, and I burst into laughter. "You know I love you, right?"

My laughter died off as I tightened my arms around his neck, bringing our bodies flush. "You show me that every day."

"Good." Our foreheads met. "I never want you to doubt it."

"I never have."

Lifting me until we were eye to eye, he said, "Where's that darn step stool when you need it?"

"You're such a jerk." I nipped at his jaw. "Now kiss me," I demanded.

And he did.

WHO SAYS WE CAN'T GET STONED?

Gideon

I T HAD BEEN ONE of those days. The kind that never seemed to end. The kind that made Gideon want to bash his head against a wall.

Rebellions in the cursed realm had started to crop up again. It was inevitable, really. There were too many Fallen and demons who did not want reform. Beelzebub was still at large, fighting to free his brothers imprisoned in Purgatory. There was finally peace between Angel and Fallen, Heaven and Hell, but the darkness could never be fully eradicated.

The universe required balance. As much as light had won the Second Battle of Heaven, the dark survived in the corners, casting ominous shadows full of promise. The tides would turn eventually. They always did.

But not today, Maker willing. Gideon was tired, and the last thing he wanted was to take up his sword and shield against the powers that plotted against them. He would, of course. When the time eventually came for another battle, Gideon would fight alongside his Committed, alongside his brothers. Because the only thing necessary for evil to win was for good men to do nothing.

Gideon questioned whether he was truly a good man at times, but he would always fight for the good of his people and, more importantly, the good of his family. He just prayed the peace lasted a little longer. Riley had seen enough war, enough pain, and Gideon wanted more for his *kapara*.

Entering the house, Gideon set aside his briefcase and smiled as Riley's laughter drifted through the air. It was high pitched, more of a giggle than a laugh. Noel's manic cackles joined him as Jai's voice barked above the noise, sounding annoyed. Those three were trouble at the best of times, and Gideon contemplated turning tail and running while he still could.

But after a day like today, he didn't want to waste time alone in his office doing paperwork or drinking at one of the Utopian pubs. He wanted to sit on the couch with Riley in his lap and maybe read a book together.

So he removed his shoes and jacket, picking up the discarded boots Jai had most likely flung to the side haphazardly upon his arrival home. How Jai was capable of keeping his bedroom tidy but still managed to clutter the rest of the house was a mystery.

Following the sounds of laughter and Jai's growing volume, Gideon found them in the family room. Noel lay on the ground, white hair fanned out over the carpet. Riley sat curled up on the couch, hugging his knees to his chest as Jai paced, his arms flailing wildly as he spoke.

"And the guy was huge, okay?" Jai was saying. "Like, massive leather Daddy. And Noel's all, 'Honey, I'mma dropkick a bitch if you don't get your hands off my Other.'" Jai pitched his voice higher to imitate Noel, and Noel shrieked with laughter.

"I did say that, didn't I?"

Jai nodded. "Yeah, 'cause you're femme as fuck when you're drunk."

Snapping his fingers three times, Noel wiggled on the ground. "Bitch, you know it," he joked, and Riley giggled into his knees.

As Gideon leaned against the doorframe, he inhaled only to cough at the lingering smoke hanging in the room. "Maker have mercy," he grunted as three pairs of glazed eyes turned his way.

"Oh shit," Noel said, blinking lazily. "Gideon's home."

"Everyone be cool," Jai said, running a hand through his hair, mussing the dark strands until they stood out in crazy directions.

"We're always cool," Riley said, snorting out another bout of giggles.

"We so are!" Noel muffled his laughter in the carpet.

Jai shook out his arms and nodded in Gideon's direction. "Hey, Gid. 'Sup, bruh."

Noel screeched. Riley covered his mouth with his hand. Jai tried to lean against the wall nonchalantly but misjudged the distance and toppled right over with a yelp.

"I might get femme as fuck when I'm trashed," Noel said, pointing at Jai. "But you get douchey."

"I do not get douchey!" Jai scrambled to his feet, expression scandalized.

"You said *bruh*." Riley shook his head in disappointment. "And *'sup*. That's douchey."

"Yeah, well, you get bratty and a little slutty," Jai said with an accusing finger pointed at Riley.

Riley gasped in affront, jaw dropping, eyes wide. "I resent that remark!"

"You mean you resemble that remark," Noel corrected, and Riley nodded vigorously.

"Yeah, I resemble that—hey! Noel!" Riley pouted as Jai and Noel guffawed.

With an exasperated sigh, Gideon approached the couch and patted the top of Riley's head. "Don't listen to them, darling. You're perfect."

Riley beamed up at him. "Aw, thanks. You, sir, are a gentleman and a scholar." He patted Gideon's stomach over his shirt, then started rubbing circles over his abs. His smile curled dangerously, and he looked up at Gideon with heavy-lidded eyes. "You should take off your shirt."

"See?" Jai waved emphatically at Riley. "Slutty!" He mimed throwing a basketball before bellowing, "Nothing but net," and doing a weird touchdown dance.

Noel and Riley pointed at him and yelled, "Douchey!"

"Saints and sinners, how am I this douchey?" Jai plopped onto the floor with a moan, cradling his head in his hands. "Do I need to reevaluate all my life's choices?"

Bringing an end to the madness, Gideon cleared his throat loudly, tugging gently on Riley's curls. "Have you been smoking salvia, *kapara*?"

Riley scrunched his nose. "Only a little."

"Oh? Just a little?" Gideon chuckled to himself as Riley nuzzled his hand like a cat. "I can't leave you three unsupervised for a moment."

"Sorry, Daddy." Noel's voice was muffled in the carpet, but Gideon heard him loud and clear.

"Ha. Daddy." Jai sniggered.

Riley smiled into Gideon's palm. "Don't be mad. My leg was hurting, and we just wanted to relax."

"I'm not mad, darling. But you need to eat and stay hydrated."

"Jai ordered pizza, but it's not here yet." Riley's lips puckered against Gideon's skin. "You smell so good. How was your day?"

"Long," Gideon answered honestly.

"I'm glad you're home." Riley pushed his cheek into Gideon's palm and smiled sweetly.

Gideon couldn't help but smile back. "So am I."

"Aw, they're so cute," Noel cooed, and Gideon glanced his way.

Jai had crawled across the floor to lie on his side between Noel's legs. His head was cushioned on Noel's ass, his arms wrapped around Noel's leg like he was hugging a body pillow. Lying on his belly, Noel propped his chin on his hands and grinned.

"Gid, are you gonna get high with us?" he asked.

Gideon shook his head. "How about I stay sober so I can take care of all of you, okay?"

"Every party needs a pooper, that's why we invited you," Jai sang, and Noel joined in. "Party pooper. That's you!"

As Riley laughed so hard he flopped over on the couch, Gideon scrubbed a hand over his face. "For Trinity's sake."

When the pizza arrived, Gideon delivered it to the three stoners in the living room. He sat on the couch beside Riley as Jai and Noel ate from their spots sprawled on the floor. He drank an ambrosia infused beer and enjoyed their stoned antics. Somehow, he allowed Riley to rope him into playing a game of charades.

"Baby!" Noel yelled as Jai pantomimed. "Baby on the ground. Rolling the baby. No, a circle. A watermelon? Oh! Oh! Watermelon baby!"

"It's *not* a baby!" Jai growled.

"No talking. That's cheating," Riley said, and Noel and Jai flipped him their middle fingers simultaneously.

"Just—watch what I'm doing." Jai continued miming the action.

"Circle. Rolling the circle. Stones. Rolling Stones!" Noel jumped up and down as Jai shook his head furiously. "Jai, how are you so bad at charades?"

"Me?" Jai propped his hands on his hips. "What the fuck is a watermelon baby?"

"I don't know. You're the one miming it!"

"Time," Gideon said, and Jai bared his teeth at his Other.

"Snowman, Noel! I'm building a fucking snowman!"

"Well, how was I supposed to know?" Noel collapsed onto the couch. "I'm too high for this."

"My turn!" Riley announced, jumping up and digging a slip of paper out of the Tupperware bowl.

As Jai and Noel bickered, Gideon sat back and watched as Riley's eyes got big. His cheeks flushed bright red, and he chewed on the inside of his cheek. He met Gideon's eyes for a moment before looking away.

"Um, okay," he muttered, setting the paper aside before moving to the center of the room.

"And..." Jai clicked the timer on his phone. "Go."

Face flushed, Riley avoided Gideon's gaze as he swayed back and forth. Gideon tried not to laugh. "Um, dancing?"

Riley spun his hand as if to say *keep going*.

"Waltz?" Gideon tried again.

"Oh my God," Riley muttered, then wriggled his body in a poor attempt at a shimmy.

"A worm?" Gideon glanced at Noel and Jai, but they, too, looked confused. Riley shook his head and wiggled again. "Caterpillar?"

"No, go back to dancing," Riley said, and Noel squealed.

"No talking!"

Holding his hands in surrender, Riley pressed his lips together and started to sway again. Gideon drained his second beer, then cleared his throat.

"Uh, interpretative dance?"

Riley shook his head, adding a more pronounced sway to his hips.

"The tango?"

"Oh my God!"

With a defeated sigh, Riley flushed a deeper shade of red before fingering the hem of his shirt. Continuing his loose sway, he smiled in embarrassment and avoided all eye contact as he started to lift his shirt up his torso. He revealed his belly button, then his lower ribs. By the time his shirt was high enough to showcase his nipples, Jai and Noel were laughing so hard they were crying.

Gideon pressed his fist to his mouth to hide his own amusement as Riley glared at them all. He whipped off his shirt completely and tossed it at Noel, who whooped and hollered like he'd just caught the bouquet at someone's wedding.

"Stripper?" Gideon said, and Riley buried his face in his hands and nodded.

"You can't get *snowman*, but Riley and Gideon manage a point for *stripper*?" Jai glowered at Noel as Riley rushed to Gideon and curled up in his lap to hide away.

"Excellent job, *kapara*," Gideon said into Riley's scalp, and Riley snickered into his chest.

Rubbing a hand up Riley's bare spine, Gideon bundled his Committed close and pecked the top of his head. Their bond pulsed warm and content between them, and Riley made a happy cooing noise in the back of his throat.

"Did you want your shirt back?" Noel asked.

Gideon would never complain about holding Riley, whether he was wearing clothes or not. Riley must have agreed because he made no move to retrieve his shirt from Noel's lap. It had been decades since Riley tried to hide his scars from them, and Gideon was happy when his Committed didn't even flinch as his palm grazed the *V*-shaped scars on his back.

When Riley's wings were out, they covered the scars, but nothing could permanently remove them. Like the scars on Noel's back, Jai's chest, and Gideon's throat and back. They were all scarred from the battles they'd fought, and though the victories were worth every blemish, there were times Gideon wished Riley had never been marked by them at all.

But that was life, he supposed. No one ever came out the other side completely untouched by tragedy or pain. It was the reality, the risk of living in this world. But if having Riley in his arms was the prize, then every risk Gideon had ever taken in his very, very long life had been worth it.

"I love you," Riley murmured into Gideon's shoulder, angling his head so he could kiss the scarred flesh of Gideon's throat.

"I love you too," Gideon said without hesitation, and when Riley scooted up enough to connect their lips in a sloppy kiss, Gideon tightened his arms around him. Riley was the most precious gift the Maker had ever given him, and Gideon would love and protect him with everything he had, everything he *was*.

Riley deepened the kiss, his tongue swiping across the seam of Gideon's mouth, but when Gideon refused him entrance, he huffed in irritation. "Giddy," he whined, and Gideon chortled.

"I think there might be a grain of truth to Jai's claims," Gideon teased. "Salvia does seem to make you rather amorous."

"Is that fancy talk for horny?" Riley asked with a roll of his eyes, and Gideon's chortle turned into a full belly laugh.

"Well, you did want me to take my shirt off."

Sitting up, Riley crossed his arms over his bare chest. "I just don't think it's fair that I'm the only shirtless one."

Jai and Noel immediately tore their shirts off and chucked them across the room, causing Riley to burst into a fit of laughter. Jai hooked an arm around Noel's neck and tugged his Other against him. Leaning his back against Jai's chest, Noel winked at Riley, using his big toe to poke him in the belly button.

Still laughing, Riley held Gideon's arm to keep his balance as he half-crawled up Noel's body to plant a kiss on Noel's plush mouth. They laughed and kissed playfully as Jai watched, an entertained smirk gracing his thin lips.

Before they got carried away, Gideon hauled Riley back into his lap, situating him sideways on his lap so Riley could rest his head on Gideon's chest and still see Jai and Noel. Riley unbuttoned Gideon's dress shirt enough to allow him access to the chest hair there. As he snuggled into Gideon, he ran his hand through the curls on his chest, utterly content.

Noel and Jai whispered to each other, exchanging a few chaste kisses that turned into a few deeper kisses. Riley watched them as Gideon watched Riley.

"They're beautiful, aren't they?" Riley mused as Jai nuzzled Noel's nose.

Gideon felt like shrugging because, as much as he could appreciate the general attractiveness of his brothers, brothers were all they would ever be to him. His heart, soul, and desires were for Riley and Riley alone.

"*You* are beautiful," Gideon said instead, and Riley turned to him with a tender smile on his lips.

"Can I sleep in your room tonight?" he asked as Noel moaned into Jai's mouth, and Gideon nodded.

"You're always welcome." He glanced at Noel and Jai as Noel shifted on the couch to straddle Jai's hips. "You don't want to join them?"

Riley considered a moment, watching his Committeds' affections grow in intensity. There was longing and heat in his gaze, but he still shook his head. "Not tonight. I wanna stay with you."

Leaving Noel and Jai on the couch, Gideon rose with Riley in his arms. Riley tightened his legs around Gideon's waist, looping his arms around his neck for stability.

"Goodnight, Noel. Goodnight, Jai," he called as Jai rolled Noel over to lie on top of him between his legs.

"Night," Noel said breathlessly. "Love you."

"Love you," Riley said as Gideon carried him out of the room.

"I'll make him scream your name, baby," Jai called out, and Gideon shook his head as Riley chuckled into his shoulder. "Love you, shortstack."

"Love you too. I'll be listening for it," Riley said, and Noel and Jai's combined laughter faded behind them as Gideon carried Riley up the stairs to his bedroom.

"You're terrible," Gideon chided lightly. "Always encouraging them."

"It's called flirting," Riley said haughtily. "It's, like, a thing."

"Oh, is that so?" Upon entering Gideon's room, he dumped Riley onto the bed in a graceless heap. "I had no idea."

"I'm getting better, you know," Riley said confidently. "At flirting."

"I'm sure you are."

As he shedded his clothing, Gideon ignored the intense way Riley watched him. His Committed's desire for him no longer made him uncomfortable, but there were still times it made him self-conscious. Even now, years and years later, Gideon still struggled with inadequacy. Old fears remained, telling him Riley would grow bored with their dynamic eventually. But that was insecurity, not truth, and Gideon would continue to remind himself of that.

"Bathe with me?" Gideon asked once he was standing in nothing but his underwear.

Riley nodded enthusiastically, scrambling from the bed and hurriedly disrobing the rest of the way. His jeans tangled around his ankles, and he yelped as he lost his balance. Gideon caught him before he hit the ground, and he snickered into Gideon's forearm.

"Oopsie-daisy." He cackled as Gideon righted him.

When Gideon knelt, Riley's hands landed on his shoulders to keep his balance. Gideon untangled Riley's feet from his pants, then removed his socks. Noel must have painted his nails recently because his tiny toes glittered pale pink and purple. Gideon liked it immensely.

Hand in hand, wearing only their underwear, they left Gideon's room and headed toward the bathroom at the end of the hall. Jai and Noel laughed in the stairwell, tripping up the steps, and Riley paused on the threshold of the bathroom as they staggered into view, disheveled and snickering.

Riley watched them with a fond smile curling his mouth, and Jai sent him a wink as he lifted Noel into his arms. Wrapping himself around Jai like an octopus, Noel giggled and finger-waved in their direction, planting a kiss on Jai's neck. Riley blew him a kiss as Gideon's Secondaries disappeared into Noel's bedroom.

With a tug on Riley's hand, Gideon guided him into the bathroom. Riley was limping, bringing Gideon's attention to his ravaged thigh. The chunk Asmodeus had taken out of Riley's leg had never regenerated, and the concave section of flesh was heavily scarred. Like Noel, Riley was in a constant state of pain. The extent of that pain differed day to day, but it lingered in the background.

Today must have been rough for him to resort to salvia just to take the edge off, and Gideon's stomach clenched. He hated when Riley was in turmoil, whether it was emotional or physical.

Riley leaned against the bathroom counter as Gideon started filling the tub with steaming water. He added some lavender bath salts, and the soothing scent permeated every corner of the small room. When the tub was full and piping hot, Gideon held out a hand expectantly, and Riley smirked, shimmying out of his underwear.

"I can get in myself," he said, but he took Gideon's hand anyway and allowed him to help him climb into the tub.

Once he was settled, Gideon removed the last of his clothing and stepped into the bathtub behind Riley. It took some situating for them to fit comfortably, but eventually, Riley settled back against Gideon's chest, his smaller body fitting between Gideon's legs snuggly. They released matching sighs as the hot water soothed away the aches of the day.

Gideon reached out and framed Riley's thigh between his big hands. Gentle but firm, he worked his fingers along the thick flesh covering the old injury. Riley hissed, tensing in Gideon's arms, but he didn't fight him. Biting his bottom lip, Riley leaned his head back onto Gideon's shoulder, eyes pinched shut as Gideon massaged the sore, ruined muscles.

"Bad day?" Gideon asked, and Riley shrugged.

"I sparred with Jesse. He needed it, and I enjoyed the practice. I just pushed too hard, I think."

Clucking his tongue in reprimand, Gideon dug his thumbs along the scarred tissue. Riley whimpered, hands dropping into the water to clutch at Gideon's thighs. His fingernails sunk into Gideon's skin, but neither of them spoke as Gideon determinedly massaged the knotted muscles.

At long last, Riley relaxed under Gideon's ministrations, exhaling long and low between pursed lips. "How are you so good at that?"

Gideon hummed dismissively as he gentled his fingers, ending the massage with light strokes up and down Riley's thighs. He kissed Riley's temple, and his Committed wriggled in his arms, pushing back against him until their bodies were flush. The water rippled around them as Riley settled more comfortably between Gideon's legs.

They sat in the warm water for ages without saying a word. It was moments such as this that Gideon treasured most. Riley in his arms, skin to skin, nothing separating them. In the quiet, their hearts fell into sync, and Gideon's soul sang.

At long last, the water began to cool, and Gideon sat up straighter. Riley remained limp in his arms, eyes drooping, a contented smile on his face. Gideon grinned and wiped damp curls from his forehead.

"Thank you," Gideon said, and Riley cocked his head.

"For what?"

"For this." Gideon squeezed Riley gently, their wet limbs entangling under the water.

"I'm just sitting here," Riley said.

With a peck to Riley's neck, right over the *G* in his tattoo, Gideon said, "Exactly."

Narrowing his eyes, Riley scrutinized Gideon for several seconds before beaming dopily up at him. "You're weird, but I'm totally into it."

"What a relief," Gideon deadpanned.

Before Gideon could stand, Riley half-turned, captured Gideon's face in his hands, and planted an exuberant kiss on his mouth. "I love you. So much."

Smiling against Riley's lips, Gideon said, "I love you too. With all I am."

"Take me to bed?" There was an undercurrent of seduction to the question, but it neither frightened or fazed Gideon.

Instead, he said simply, "It would be my honor."

And later, as Riley lay curled against Gideon's side, breathing deeply, Gideon counted his many blessings, the most important of which slept tranquilly in his arms. Gideon had lived many years plagued by regret, but every mistake and struggle had led him here. To this moment, lying entwined with his Committed.

If he'd known at the start where it would take him, Gideon was sure he would make the same choices. For this life, he would live every pain and heartache over again. For Riley, he would give everything anew. Because Riley was worth it all.

For the first time in Gideon's very long life, he was at peace. He was completely and perfectly and incandescently happy. And happiness, he'd found out, suited him just fine.

BY POPULAR DEMAND

Riley

T HE EVENING SUN WAS hot on my skin, and I adjusted my sunglasses as the sand underneath my towel shifted. Waves crashed against the shore, and the wind carried the faraway sound of Noel's laughter to my ears. Eyes still closed, I smiled and exhaled a long, contented breath.

Jai barked something unintelligible, and Noel screeched. Much closer, the page of a book turned with a crisp scratch, and I cracked an eye open to peer to my left. Gideon sat in a plastic lounge chair, half-reclined, his sunglasses propped on top of his head as his reading glasses rested on the bridge of his nose. An umbrella stood tall behind him, casting his upper body in shadow as he read.

As if he felt my gaze, he glanced down at me lying on the sand just out of reach of the umbrella's shadow. He cocked a dark blond eyebrow. I smiled up at him. His dimple waved hello as the corner of his mouth lifted minutely. I settled back on my beach towel as Gideon returned his attention to his book.

Our silent exchange lasted mere seconds, but the Committed bond between us glowed brightly for minutes after.

Jai and Noel were somewhere in the ocean, swimming in the waters of the Arabian Sea. Joy and adrenaline zipped through our bonds as they snorkeled, and I basked in the overwhelming happiness that radiated between the four of us.

These moments of relaxation and peace were growing fewer and farther apart as our responsibilities multiplied. But when I'd finally agreed to have an official Commitment ceremony, I'd been adamant at getting some sort of honeymoon out of it. My angels hadn't put up much of a fight, and the plans had begun.

The ceremony itself had been an intimate affair, attended by only our closest friends. Now that it was over, I grudgingly admitted that it had been a beautiful and loving experience, but I'd be lying if I said I hadn't been resistant.

Not because I didn't want to be Committed to my angels in every possible way, but because it seemed unnecessary. Not to mention, I had to stand up in front of people and be the center of attention for an extended period of time. I loved being the sole focus of my angels, but being stared at by others still made my skin itch.

But the ceremony had been important to them—Gideon and Noel, specifically—so I had relented. Jai didn't care one way or another; he shared my sentiments for the most part. We were bonded, and we'd been living together for decades. What difference did one ceremony make? Yet it had meant something to Gideon and Noel, and when it came down to it, I would give them anything and everything their hearts desired.

So I'd stood with my angels in front of our friends in a public display of our Commitment. We'd shared a glass of wine, then braided a cord of four ropes together while Nadia sang a traditional Utopian bonding song. They'd offered me their swords one at a time, repeating traditional Utopian vows, and then it had been my turn.

Wedding rings were a human symbol, not an angelic one, but since I'd grown up in the human world, it meant something to me all the same. I had chosen their rings and engraved *"Ani l'dodi v'dodi li"* inside each of the bands. And one by one, I had slipped them on their fingers, stammering through my own vows, personalized for each of my loves.

It had been sappy and a little awkward with four of us shifting around each other to make room for the others, but in the end, it had been a wonderful moment.

Gideon had worn Utopian ceremonial robes, while Jai dawned a simpler tunic and trouser ensemble that was heavily embroidered with dark threads that resembled the lines of ink embedded in his skin. Noel, naturally, had looked the most bridal in a silky, gender neutral outfit made up of tight leggings, a sheer skirt overtop, and flowing material draped around his bare torso and arms. His hair had sparkled like opals, fresh flowers woven through the white strands.

I'd worn a suit—simple slacks, a pale yellow shirt, and a blazer. To an outsider, it had probably looked chaotic and un-planned, but for us, it worked. We'd never been what anyone considered normal, and our Commitment ceremony wasn't either. But to us, it was pretty close to perfect.

And now, we were on our honeymoon, lying under the Goan sun as the Indian Ocean crashed over the shores of India's south-west coast. We'd rented a house on a private beach where we could swim, snorkel, and sunbathe without interruption. We stayed up late and slept in later. We walked to the beach town restaurants to eat fresh seafood and authentic Indian curries. Some nights, we'd drink too much and get into all sorts of shenanigans that Gideon would lecture us about in the morning. Other nights, we'd settle in for a quiet night with a movie or a good book. Secret moments were stolen, witnessed only by the pale, Indian moon or the crabs scurrying over the rocks.

Our first night, Jai had woken me when the sky was at its darkest, and we'd gone for a midnight swim. Bathed in moonlight, we'd made love in the warm waters, Jai's teeth marking my neck as my hands circled us both, stroking us to completion. When exploring the rocks and caves near our rental, Noel had shoved me into a dark corner, yanked down my board shorts, and proceeded to eat me out until I came against the rocks with his tongue inside me and his fingers wrapped around my shaft.

Waking Gideon before the sun, I had led him out onto the beach where we sat—me curled up between his legs as his arms engulfed me completely—as the sky lightened. Pinks and purples, yellows and oranges streaked the sky, and as the sun peeked above the horizon, Gideon tightened his hold around me and placed a tender kiss to the nape of my neck.

"The universe is full of miracles," he'd murmured as we watched the sunrise, "but you're the most precious one of all."

His lips had been firm but gentle when I'd craned my neck to kiss him.

And now, the time in our slice of personal heaven was drawing to a close. Our lives and responsibilities in Utopia awaited us, and we would have to return. But not yet. We still had time, and I was going to soak up every second and commit it to memory. I never wanted to forget what this felt like.

Jai and Noel's voices were significantly louder now, and I sat up, sliding my sunglasses to the top of my head as they walked out of the water side by side. I admired the view as the evening sunlight played over their drenched skin. Sea water trickled down their muscled chests, and they seemed to glisten and glow against the backdrop of the setting sun.

It was unfair how attractive they were, but since they were all mine, I figured I could live with the injustice.

"You're drooling," Gideon teased as he turned another page, never taking his eyes off his book.

"If you were gay, you would be too," I retorted, and a loud laugh burst out of him, surprising us both.

"Maker help me." He removed his reading glasses and scrubbed a hand over his face as he chuckled. "The things that come out of your mouth."

Feeling playful and a bit naughty, I said, "They're not nearly as scandalous as the things that go into my mouth."

Gideon shot me a chiding look, and I stuck out my tongue in retaliation.

Jai plopped down beside me, cool water from his body splashing onto my sun-baked arm, and said, "Do I want to know why you're talking about things that go into Riley's mouth?"

"Ooh." Noel forced his way onto my towel, and I parted my legs so he could shimmy between them. "That might be one of my favorite topics."

"Maker give me strength," Gideon muttered as the rest of us laughed.

I scooched forward until I was pressed to Noel's back from chest to groin. Hooking my chin over his shoulder, I circled his waist and linked my fingers over his belly button.

"How was the water?" I kissed his shoulder blade, and he leaned back into me, blanketing my hands with his.

"We saw a shark."

"And Noel screamed like a baby," Jai added.

Affronted, Noel chucked a handful of sand at Jai's chest. "I did not!"

"So I rode in, like a knight in shining armor, and saved him," Jai finished, attempting to brush away the sand. Because he was wet, the sand merely smeared over his tattooed torso and coated his hands. He wrinkled his nose, then shrugged, lying back in the sand without a care.

"I don't need rescuing," Noel sniffed haughtily. "And if I did, I would want Riley to rescue me."

Glancing over his shoulder, Noel beamed at me, and I tilted my head up in silent request. He answered with a kiss to my lips. He tasted like salt and sun, and I bit back a groan when he wiggled his butt against my groin, his tongue teasing the seam of my mouth.

"If sand didn't get everywhere…" Noel drifted off, leaving my imagination to fill in the rest.

"You'd be good and not risk getting arrested for public indecency?" Gideon finished Noel's sentence with a lofty air, and Noel smiled innocently at him.

"Of course, Gideon. What did you think I meant?"

Jai laughed, his teeth gleaming white against his dark skin and even darker facial hair. "What's the point of renting a private beach if we can't risk a little public indecency?"

I hid my amusement against Noel's spine as Gideon harrumphed. But his dimple was visible, and his eyes were shining, so I knew he wasn't seriously offended by Jai and Noel's unseemly antics.

When my stomach growled, we packed up our beach equipment and made the short trek back to the bungalow. Gideon had thrown together a light meal earlier that afternoon, and we ate outside on the uneven planks of the front porch. Noel's hair dried in tangles, the caked salt making the strands thick. My own curls were in chaotic disarray, made worse by the sand, and Jai's black hair stuck up in eight different directions.

"We should shower together," Jai said in a no-nonsense tone, "to conserve water."

Noel nodded solemnly. "Yes, to conserve water. We should do our part for the environment."

"Sex has nothing to do with it, of course," Gideon called from the kitchen where he was rinsing the plates, and I choked on my drink.

"Why does Gideon think we're sex-crazed deliquents?" Noel demanded.

"Might have something to do with you ruining our couch," Jai said.

"With your cum," I added in a whisper.

Noel flushed. "That was your fault! I still can't believe I'm the only one who took the fall for it."

With a satisfied grin, I leaned back and twined my fingers behind my head. "The perks of sleeping with the boss."

A drop of silence, then Noel and Jai burst into raucous laughter as Gideon shouted, "I heard that!"

I showered, managing to wash myself and my hair before Jai and Noel piled into the tiny bathroom with me. I let them kiss me and run soapy, wet hands over my body, but I slipped out from between them before we got too carried away.

"Where are you going?" Jai growled as Noel wrinkled his face in disappointment.

"Get clean, then come find me," I said mysteriously, and Noel grinned. Jai's dangerous expression sent a shiver down my spine, and I turned my back on them and waltzed naked out of the bathroom.

Wearing nothing but a pair of Jai's boxers, I padded through the two-bedroom bungalow, finding Gideon in the kitchen. He was still shirtless from our afternoon on the beach, and I embraced him from behind, burying my face in his strong back. Since he hadn't swam, he didn't smell like salt or fish. He smelled like sand and sunshine and peppermint. I inhaled deeply, then pressed my lips to the scar on his back.

"Hello, darling," he said as he set his glass of wine aside. "I thought you three would be longer."

A blush heated my cheeks at his insinuation. "I'm playing a long game tonight."

"Torturing them?"

"I don't torture them," I snorted into his spine. "Just making them work for it."

"Good man."

Gideon turned in my hold, and my chin came to a rest on his sternum. His eyes were so impossibly green, and the love glittering in the depths made my throat thick and tight.

"I love you," I said, and he cupped my face so gently, like he was afraid, even after all this time, that he would break me.

Instead of replying with words, he bent down and kissed me. It was sweet and tender until his tongue slithered into my mouth, deepening the kiss. Our tongues twisted, and I shivered as his huge hands dragged down my neck and around to my back. He traced my scars reverently as I ran my fingers through his thick chest hair.

By the time we parted, I was panting, and Gideon's face was flushed. I'd been half-hard since leaving two of my Committeds naked and wet in the shower, but after a kiss like that, I was tenting my underwear obscenely. Gideon didn't mind. He glanced down at my obvious erection and smiled.

"Shall I send you back to Jai and Noel to take care of that?" he asked in a teasing tone.

Mimicking the lightness, I said, "Only if you join us."

He chuckled, but when I didn't share in his amusement, his laughter faded. His brows drew down as the smile dissolved from his face. We stared at each other for a never-ending moment before he stepped back, physically distancing himself from me.

"Riley—"

"You could watch," I blurted, heat sweltering in my cheeks. "You could—I mean, it's okay if your answer is no. I just... there's a divide, and I thought, maybe, there wouldn't have to be. You can be with us in whatever way you want."

He shook his head. "I don't see them that way. You know that."

"Okay." I bridged the gap between us and took his hand. "I'm not trying to push. I just want to make sure you know that the invitation is there. You don't have to stay away. You don't have to stay separate if you don't want to."

I squeezed his hand, silently asking if we were okay, and he squeezed back in reassurance. "I know *you* feel this way, but they may not."

Before I could respond, Noel spoke up behind me. "We do."

Gideon's fingers twitched in my hold as his attention jumped up and over my shoulder. I turned, following his gaze to where Jai and Noel stood in the mouth of the hallway leading to the bedrooms. Noel wore one of Gideon's shirts, though it wasn't as huge on him as it was on me. The hem tickled the tops of his thighs, unable to cover his briefs completely. Jai leaned against the wall, arms crossed over his chest as his sweatpants hung low on his hips. I could see the barest hint of his pubic hair—he wasn't wearing underwear, and it did terrible, amazing things to me.

"We told you from the start that we wanted you as involved as you wanted to be," Noel continued, tucking a chunk of his white hair behind his ear. "What that looks like is entirely up to you. If there are aspects to this"—he waved his hand at all four of us—"that you want no part in, we will always respect that."

"But you don't have to stand apart just because you think you're not wanted," Jai finished, and my heart swelled. "You can share this with us, even if you don't actually want to fuck us," he added just to be obnoxious, and the fuzzies in my stomach crashed and burned.

"Classy," I deadpanned, and Jai winked at me.

Noel bit his bottom lip to stave off a laugh, and I chanced a peek at Gideon. His brow was furrowed, but it was his thinking-face not his offended-face. We were quiet for almost a full minute as Gideon pondered what we'd said. His thumb tapped against my hand, an absent gesture, and the bond between us was oddly still.

"I don't... know," he finally said. "I'm going to shower and think about it."

"Okay," I said, trying not to let the tension in my gut show on my face. "Take as much time as you need."

His smile was fleeting and didn't reach his eyes, but he did lean down and peck my lips before he dropped my hand and lumbered past Jai and Noel toward the bathroom. We watched him go, none of us speaking until the bathroom door shut and the pipes started to rattle.

"Well, that could have gone worse," Noel said, running a hand through his damp hair.

"Could have gone better," Jai parried.

"Sorry if I spoke out of turn." I leaned on the counter and released the breath I'd subconsciously been holding. "It just kind of spilled out. I didn't mean to put either of you on the spot or—"

"Riles, if we had an issue, we'd say so," Jai said.

Noel nodded in agreement. "We all have different boundaries, and as long as we communicate those, it'll work out."

"I don't think he'll ever want to..." I started but stopped myself. "It's not my place to even pretend to know, let alone predict what Gideon wants. I just see the way he automatically pulls away when the three of us are together, and I want to make sure it's his choice, not because he's assuming he's not welcome, you know?"

"Well, you told him. Now it's up to him to figure out what that can mean for him." Noel held out his hand expectantly, and I shoved off the counter, closed the distance between us, and slipped my hand into his. Palm to palm, he drew me in and kissed me lightly. "Hopefully, it means we can share this together in whatever way we're all comfortable with."

"I like when he watched us," I confessed quietly. "I think maybe he'd like to watch sometimes, and it would be a way for all of us to share this."

Jai's fingers circled the back of my neck firmly. "But you have to be okay if that's not something Gideon wants."

"I know," I said, because I did. "I just didn't want it to go unsaid."

"It's okay to want things, even if they may not happen," Noel said kindly.

"Just be realistic because I don't want you to get your hopes up," Jai added.

I nodded and tilted my head back until our gazes met. "I love you."

The embers in Jai's eyes burned brighter, and he smiled. "Love you too, shortstack."

"And me? What about me?" Noel grabbed my chin and forced me to look at him.

Laughing, I tightened my arms around his waist and said, "I love you too. Always."

"Always," he echoed before kissing me again, with more purpose this time.

We kissed in the hallway, me trapped between them as our hands wandered. Our bonds crackled and thrummed, and I closed my eyes to focus on every touch and caress. Jai's fingers were callused and rough, Noel's soft and tender. Teeth grazed my ear as a hand cupped my erection, massaging determinedly.

"Should we wait for him?" Noel asked as I sucked on his pulse point.

"Wouldn't that be putting extra pressure on him," Jai rasped around my earlobe.

"Let's go to the bedroom, but leave the door open," I gasped out, rolling my hips into Noel's hand. "If he wants to join, he can without it being a thing."

That was all the encouragement they needed. We stumbled down the hall, groping and kissing, laughing and teasing. It was like we were young again.

Life changed and molded us, and sometimes, we got swept up in routine. Our love was as strong as ever, but it was nice to rekindle the fire every now and then. As we tripped into the master bedroom with the king-sized bed, I felt giddy and almost nervous, like I was that inexperienced boy again.

"What do you want?" Jai asked with a tug on my curls. "Tell us what you want, Riles."

"Both of you," I said, confident and unashamed.

Noel groaned into the back of Jai's neck, his eyes darkening to violet over his Other's shoulder. "Are you sure? It might scare Gideon off forever."

"I want both of you," I repeated, and Jai's responding grin was almost feral.

"Hands on the bed," he ordered. "You'll need to be good and stretched."

Shivering, I obeyed him. I bent at the waist at the foot of the bed and placed my palms on the mattress. Noel dragged his hands down my spine, fingers hooking in the band of my underwear and sliding them down my legs. When his hands spread me open, his stare prickled along my flesh, but there was no time for the embarrassment to set in. His mouth was on me immediately, and I half-yelped, half-shouted at the assault.

Jai shuffled around somewhere behind us, gathering supplies as Noel rimmed me. I was hard as steel now, and I fisted my hands in the blanket and rocked back against Noel's mouth. I could have come from this alone, but he backed off before the pleasure could truly build.

Noel was replaced by Jai, and I startled when two fingers, covered in cold lube, probed at the ring of muscles Noel's tongue had been trying to loosen. Those callused fingers were rough, but Jai knew my body better than I did sometimes. He pushed just shy of too much, until the quasi-pain sent pleasure singing through my veins.

"Oh God," I whimpered, lowering myself until my face was buried in the mattress.

Noel's hand caressed my hair as Jai opened me up enough for the plug. It was big, meant to stretch me wider than normal to accommodate what we were about to do. It wasn't comfortable, but if I wanted them both inside me, I needed to properly prepare for it.

The plug pushed against my hole, and I bore down to pave the way. It was slow-going, and I breathed through the discomfort as the widest part of the plug stretched me.

"You're doing so well," Noel cooed, kissing the side of my head.

"Fuck, Riley, look at you. Taking it so good." The pressure eased as Jai withdrew the plug slightly, then pushed it back in. Back and forth, each time smoother than the last until the plug was fully seated inside me.

I groaned, feeling much too full, but my heart leapt when Jai said, "Good boy."

"You okay?" Noel checked in, a gentle hand cupping my hip. "Any pain?"

There was always discomfort at first, the pinching pain of penetration, but it was already fading. "I'm fine," I said, voice muffled by the bed.

Chuckling, Jai pecked my tailbone, and Noel squeezed my hip.

As my body adjusted to the overwhelming intrusion, I slowly straightened. The plug shifted deeper, rubbing against my prostate, and I shuddered.

Kneeling on the bed, Noel shifted until he was in front of me and captured my lips in an intense kiss. Jai's body warmed my back as his hands mapped my skin, trailing fingers over my shoulders and down my arms. I let them distract me from the discomfort down below.

"He may need more convincing," Noel whispered against my lips. "You up for it, sweetheart?"

Intelligently, I said, "Hmm?"

With his hands on my shoulders, Jai turned me to face the doorway where Gideon stood, white-knuckling the door-jamb. His eyes were bright, X-raying right through me, and desire pulsed in my every nerve-ending. Like the first time he'd played voyeur to Noel and I, he looked ready to bolt.

"Are you hurt?" he demanded, voice rough and deep. I shook my head, and he frowned. "That looked like it hurt."

Since my brain was overloaded and most of my blood was flowing south, I had to take an extra second to find words. "A little pain is okay."

Gideon looked away, and I took the reprieve to gather my thoughts. Turning to Jai, I said, "Give me a minute?"

"Of course."

"Will you suck Noel for me?" I asked, and he smiled like a shark.

He didn't reply with words, but his hand at my throat and the hard way he kissed me were answer enough. He broke the earth-shattering kiss, then slapped my butt, purposefully jostling the plug inside me. Whining, I glowered as he saun-tered toward the bed where Noel was still kneeling, cheeks pink, pupils blown out. He looked debauched, and we'd barely gotten started.

As Jai made quick work of stripping Noel, I faced Gideon again and approached. I probably looked silly trying to walk with a huge plug in my butt as my erection bobbed, but Gideon didn't seem to notice. His attention was on my face as I came to a stop in front of him.

Taking his hand, I gently tugged him into the room. Every step was a question, and he answered each one hesitantly. But still, he answered. He let me lead him to a chair in the corner near the dresser, and when I guided him to sit, he obeyed.

He wore his pajama pants, but his hair was still wet, the ends swollen and dripping water onto his shoulders. I tracked a droplet as it wriggled down his scarred throat, between his pecs, through his chest hair, then over the ridges of his abdomen. I collected it on my fingers before it was absorbed in the waistband of his pajama bottoms.

Silently, I crawled into his lap, trying to hide my wince as the plug's position was, once again, upset. But Gideon caught it, and his frown deepened.

"I'm fine," I reiterated as Noel moaned behind me. I resisted the urge to turn and watch Jai at work. "I need to be stretched for what we want to do. It's uncomfortable, but my body will adjust. It's okay."

"You shouldn't hurt yourself," he muttered, almost like he was sulking.

"It's not... it's a very specific kind of hurt. But then it stops hurting, and it feels good." I cupped his cheek as his massive hands framed my waist. "I know what my body can take. Trust me."

"You know I do," he said, and I smiled.

Noel took up a chorus of curse words, and Gideon laughed awkwardly. Naked and obviously turned on, I flushed and laughed with him. One hand on his cheek, the other on his chest over his heart, I leaned in and pressed my forehead to his.

"Is this okay?" I asked. Gideon swallowed audibly, his fingers flexing, then relaxing against my skin. "If you need to leave, if it gets too much, it's okay. If this isn't what you want, that's okay too. I don't want you to force yourself to stay if you don't want this."

"You're beautiful," he murmured, thumbs pressing. "Your pleasure is beautiful. I don't know how this... it may not be..."

A cruel part of me enjoyed when Gideon fumbled with his words, because it made him more adorably human to me, but I saved him this time. "It's okay. This is about communicating and enjoying being together, no matter what that looks like. We define who we are to each other; we define what this looks like. Right?"

Gideon's mouth on mine was all the answer I got, and I clutched at his broad shoulders, moaning against his lips as my erection rubbed over his abs. My moans harmonized with Noel's and I heard a distant, "If you don't stop, I'm going to come before I even get inside him!"

It broke the moment between Gideon and I, and we laughed as we parted. Jai snapped something back at Noel, and they bickered in hushed tones as Gideon rumbled his quiet humor. I bit my bottom lip and hugged him tightly.

"*Ani ohev otcha*," I said.

"Ani ohev otcha," he returned. "Now, go let them love you."

Crawling off his lap, I held eye contact as I backed up toward the bed. When I finally turned away from him, I found Noel straddling Jai's hips, his hands working their erections in tandem as Jai sucked one of Noel's pink nipples into his mouth. They were so beautiful together, and I took a moment to admire them before I climbed onto the bed and knee-walked to them.

I kissed Noel's plush mouth as Jai rolled his tongue piercing over Noel's nipple, and my fair angel keened, rocking in Jai's lap. "Hellfire, I'm not gonna last," he complained, and I wrenched his hands away from his and Jai's erections. He made a noise of protest, but I kissed it off his lips as I manhandled him onto his back and fit myself between his legs.

When our hard lengths met, we both groaned, and it was a mad flurry of limbs to get us in position. Lying diagonal across the bed, Noel looked up at me as I straddled his waist. Jai shifted behind us, and I glanced over my shoulder to watch him slick Noel with lube. Then I faced forward and met Gideon's uncertain, but awed gaze.

Jai worked the plug inside me until I was panting, my shaft an angry red color as it dripped onto Noel's stomach. Noel circled my tip with his finger, murmuring encouragements up at me as Jai added a finger beside the plug. Then it was two fingers, and I hissed at the stretch.

"Breathe," Noel said.

"Relax," Jai said.

I said, "More."

When the plug popped out of me, I felt empty and bereft, but it lasted only a moment. Because Jai was guiding me back, and Noel was thrusting up and into me in one smooth glide. Cursing in Utopian, Noel's eyes closed as he bottomed out, and I sat up straight, letting him settle deep.

And Gideon watched, a subtle blush on his cheeks.

Without breaking eye contact, I rolled my hips, taking my pleasure from Noel inside me. I lifted up and sat back down, meeting Noel's thrusts. A constant hum of pleasure streamed from his mouth as I rode him, but I still didn't look away from Gideon.

Lost in Gideon's eyes, I didn't notice Jai's fingers joining Noel inside me until his other hand splayed over my back and pushed me forward. Lying down chest to chest with Noel, I met his purple eyes.

"Hi," he breathed out.

"Hey." I kissed him as the head of Jai's erection nudged against where Noel and I were joined. "Oh."

"Breathe," he reminded me, and I breathed out, long and low.

Then Jai was slowly pushing in, and I lost my breath completely. I tried not to let the pain show on my face, but I winced as I was stretched wider than I'd ever been stretched before. A guttural noise scraped my throat, and Noel trembled under me with the effort of remaining motionless.

It seemed to take ages for Jai to work himself inside me to join Noel, but finally, *finally*, he was there. I cried out, burying my face in Noel's neck. Noel's fingers dug into my thighs as Jai's hand rubbed soothing circles over my back.

"Riley, you good?" Jai asked, and my God, he sounded wrecked.

I couldn't speak. It was so much.

"Riles? What color?" he demanded.

"Yellow," I ground out, and his fingers on my back twitched. "I need a minute. I just—oh my God, it's a lot."

"Jai," Noel sounded worried, and for a moment, it felt like Jai was going to pull out.

"No!" I reached back and clamped a hand on Jai's bare thigh. "Don't go. Just a minute. I need a minute."

"Okay," Jai said, voice strained and rough, like his throat was full of gravel. "Deep breaths, baby."

Noel peppered my shoulder with kisses, his hand massaging the back of my neck as I burrowed into his throat, inhaling lilac and dokha and sweat. And peppermint. Because Gideon was here too. We were all together.

It was overwhelming, and my eyes stung, emotion swelling within me until I felt I would burst. A broken sob lurched from my chest, and worry zipped through our bonds. Noel's and Jai's. And Gideon's.

"I love you," I choked out. "I love you all so much."

Noel held me tighter as Jai grasped my hips hard enough to leave marks. And a third hand, thick fingers shy but determined, whispered through my curls. I looked up, blinking through tears, and Gideon smiled at me. He crouched at the end of the bed near Noel's head and ran his fingers through my sweaty hair.

"You are everything we could ever have hoped for, *kapara*," he said, each word punctuated by Noel's lips on my neck and Jai's thumbs *pressing*. "There is no other."

Jai shifted on his knees, and both Noel and I cried out. Gideon's fingers tightened in my hair, stopping my head from falling forward as Jai started to carefully, gently rock his hips. My eyes nearly rolled back into my head, but I was arrested by Gideon's emerald stare.

He didn't let go of my hair.

Not when Jai started thrusting in earnest, nails carving into my skin. Not when Noel dissolved into a mumbling, keening mess beneath me. Not when I lost control of my tongue and babbled incoherent declarations of love and devotion. Not even when I said, "More. Please, I—oh my God, I'm gonna—holy cats!"

The orgasm that wracked through me hit with the weight of a freight train. Jai and Noel were right there with me, and we glowed together, swirling in the maelstrom of pleasure. It was Jai's; it was Noel's; it was mine. And... it was Gideon's. Because he was glowing with us.

It wasn't the same, but he was a tangible presence in the storm, and I clung to the anchor he offered desperately. We tumbled and fell.

We thought, "Ours. This is ours."

We thought, "Here. Here. *Here*. We were always meant to be here."

We thought, "Maybe we don't deserve this, but we will never give it up."

We thought, "Thank you," and "I love you," and "Finally. *Finally!*"

Then the glow dissipated, and our ties unwound, and we were four separate people again.

I was sprawled across Noel's chest, our torsos stuck together by the embarrassing amount of cum I'd spilled between us. Jai curled over my back, still on his knees somehow and supporting his weight with one hand on Noel's thigh, the other on my back. Eyes closed, a love-drunk smile on his face, Noel laughed and moaned as his flagging erection twitched inside me.

And Gideon, still crouched beside us, brushing his thumb over the curls plastered to my sweaty forehead. He was smiling at me, expression peaceful, eyes content. I tried to grin back, but I had a feeling it looked delirious. I felt delirious, like

I wasn't quite connected to my body yet, but it didn't scare me. My Committeds were here, and they would never let anything happen to me.

Unafraid, I drifted in the tranquil aftermath of our love, trusting my angels to keep me from floating away completely.

HIDE & SEEK

Riley

"**N**OEL, ARE YOU ALMOST ready?" I called into the house as I slipped on my shoes. "They're gonna be done at the market before we even get there at this rate."

"Don't be dramatic!" Noel shouted back from his bedroom.

I checked my watch. I wasn't being dramatic; he was taking forever. "Noel—"

"I'm here, okay?" He stomped into the hallway, dressed in skinny jeans and a crop top. "Don't blame me for us being late. You're the one who wanted to fuck in the kitchen while the house was empty."

Jumping from one foot to the other, Noel tugged on his ankle boots, and I chuckled. "You didn't seem to mind."

"I never mind when you want me to fuck you, *ahuvi*. I only mind when you get snippy at me about the time when you're the reason I had to change my clothes."

With a naughty smirk, he sauntered toward me, and I placed my hands on his waist the moment he was within touching distance. I traced the bare skin the crop top revealed, and he nuzzled my nose with his.

"I'm sorry," I said. "I wasn't trying to be snippy."

"I'm sure you can make it up to me somehow," he purred.

"I'm not letting you paint me naked," I said sternly, and Noel pouted.

"You're no fun at all."

Capturing my face in his hands, he leaned down and kissed me deeply. I could still taste the salty hint of my orgasm on his tongue, and I smiled against his mouth. He hummed, pressing us together as his fingers delved into my curls, but our kiss was interrupted by the front door bursting open, banging against the wall hard enough to rattle the walls. It startled us both, and we jerked apart to investigate.

"Addie? Where are you?" Jai bellowed, rushing past us without so much as a glance in our direction.

Noel's eyes widened, and he scrambled after Jai. Fear tightened in my chest as I limped after them both, following Jai's near-hysterical cries.

"Adalaide, this isn't funny! You tell Papa where you are right now." Jai almost barreled Noel over as he backtracked down the stairs. "Fuck!"

"What's wrong?" Noel demanded as Jai scrubbed a hand over his bearded face. His hair stood on end like he'd been tugging on it. His eyes roared with a furious inferno. "Jairus?"

"I lost her," he said, voice shaking. He met my gaze, stricken. "She was right beside me. I let go of her hand for one second."

Noel was gone in a flash, taking the stairs two at a time as he shouted for our daughter. "Addie? Baby? We don't want to play hide and seek right now. Can you come out?"

"She was right there." Jai shoved his hands in his hair as I framed his face with my hands, smelling dokha and leather.

"Breathe," I said, and he breathed. "Where's Gideon?"

"I didn't see him in the crowd. I thought maybe she headed home—"

"She wouldn't have come home alone." I tugged him down and pressed a comforting, fleeting kiss to his lips. "We'll find her."

"I'm sorry," he said. "I just let go of her for a second."

"She's four. A second is all she needs to cause an uproar. But everyone knows her; we'll find her." I squeezed the fiery thread stretched between me and Gideon. *Home, home, home,* I said through the bond, and I felt a confused, but unconcerned, ripple ping through the bond. "Gideon's on his way. We'll make some calls."

Noel charged down the stairs. "She's not upstairs in any of her normal hiding spots." His voice was high with panic. "Did you check the garden?"

"Stop panicking," I said. When had I become the most level-headed out of the three of us? Parenting did strange things to people. "She's probably batting her eyelashes for free sweets at the market. She's not going to get lost in Utopia."

"How are you this calm? It's like you don't even care," Jai snarled, and I stumbled back a step like he'd hit me. He paled instantly. "I didn't mean—"

"She's my daughter too, you prick," I snapped before limping toward the front door. Stress always made the pain in my thigh flare up. Coupled with the rigorous kitchen sex, the ache was almost enough to have me reaching for my cane at the door. I didn't.

"Riles." Jai hauled me back against him, my back to his chest. His breath was hot on my ear. "I'm sorry. You know I didn't mean that."

I did, but it still hurt. From the moment Addie was born, Noel had taken to parenthood like a fish to water. Jai had been nervous, hesitant, but he'd cried the first time she curled her tiny fingers around his thumb. It took weeks before he felt comfortable holding her or tending to her without Noel or Gideon there, but he'd been lost to her from the start.

Gideon was as gentle and loving to our child as he was with me. He'd held her first, this giant man gazing at the tiny, wrinkled creature in his arms with adoration. To everyone's shock, I'd been the one who'd taken the longest to adjust.

It was selfishness, pure and simple. For over fifty years, I'd been the center of our universe, and I'd loved every second. Then Addie arrived, and I was shoved out of the way. I was mortified to admit how bitter I'd been. A grown adult, jealous of a baby. Pathetic.

But I had adjusted. I'd gotten over my irrational insecurities and fears, and now I couldn't imagine our life without our daughter. I loved her like she was a piece of me, and the fear that she was lost and alone threatened to cripple me—more than I was already crippled. The first time she got sick, I'd held her for hours, terrified that my bitterness had caused it, that it was my fault she was in pain.

Even now, I felt guilty every time something bad happened to her, like I'd inadvertently cursed her as a baby by my near rejection. Jai knew this; they all did. Somehow, they loved me enough to forgive me for my selfish ego, encouraging me to be the father I was terrified I could never be. I'd never had a dad, and I felt like I was faking my way through the ins and outs of parenting, positive I was traumatizing our daughter in some form or fashion.

It was cruel of Jai, but that was the risk of loving someone so completely. They knew exactly where to hit to make it hurt the worst. But I also knew Jai as thoroughly as he knew me. When he was afraid, he lashed out, and nothing scared him more than Addie being lost or hurt.

"Baby, forgive me," he whispered into my temple, kissing me softly. "I'm sorry."

"I know." I looked up and smiled tightly. "It's fine. Let's just go find her."

Taking Noel's hand, I walked out of the house that we'd lived in for the past five years. It was bigger than our first one to accommodate the extra family member. Gideon and Jai had built a swingset out back, and the front yard was littered with kid toys. Addie had an entire playroom connected to her bedroom that Noel had painstakingly painted into a forest wonderland. Our daughter was probably the most spoiled child in the realm with four doting fathers.

Against all logic, I was the strict parent. Gideon was firm and fair, but even he had a weakness for her pout and crocodile tears. Sometimes I feared I was too strict, like I was turning into Ms. Janet. It was my biggest fear; I never wanted to hurt Addie the way Janet hurt me. But I trusted my angels to never let that happen. Thank God they were on my team.

My feet had barely made contact with the street when Jai released a guttural groan of relief. Noel gasped, and the tightness in my chest eased as I caught sight of a large, lumbering man leading a tiny figure by the hand. Gideon and Adelaide had almost the exact same shade of dark blond hair, though Addie's was always a frizzy, curly mess. She resembled her mother that way.

When one of my foolhardy students, Peter, had impregnated a human girl, he'd shown up on our doorstep in a panic. Addie's mother had been in college at the time, and babies—especially supernatural ones—were not in her plan. Peter was young and unprepared. Noel had met with him and explained how the adoption process would work if both he and the girl decided they didn't want the baby.

Of course, the moment they officially signed to give up their parental rights, Noel had sat us all down and practically begged us to consider adopting the Nephalem. Or half-Hybrid? Not that it mattered what she was; she was our daughter now, and we loved her more than we'd loved anything in the entire universe.

As Gideon and Addie approached, we walked to meet them. Jai squeezed the back of my neck before rushing in front of us and dropping to his knees as Addie broke away from Gideon and pumped her little legs as fast as they could go. She threw her little body into Jai's waiting arms, and my tough angel's breath hitched.

"Don't you ever do that to me again, Adalaide Isabella!" he half-shouted. "Do you have any idea how worried I've been? I couldn't find you. Why did you walk away from me? You know better than that."

I was close enough now to see the tears welling in her green eyes as Jai shook her gently by the shoulders. "But I was with *Abba*," she said wetly.

Just like that, Jai's face crumpled. "Oh, baby, don't cry. Papa's not mad. I promise. I was just scared. I didn't know you were with Abba."

Rubbing the back of his neck, Gideon cringed. "She said you knew she was with me."

With a dismissing wave, Jai drew her back into an embrace, smothering her wet cheeks with kisses. "You need to tell me next time, okay?"

"I'm sowwy, Papa." Peeking at Noel and me over Jai's shoulder, she sniffled and whispered, "Is *Ima* and Daddy mad at me?"

A broken sound escaped Noel's throat as he knelt down beside Jai and opened his arms to Addie. "No, darling, Ima's not mad. Come here."

He rocked Addie back and forth, whispering reassurances in her ear as she twisted a chunk of his long hair around her fist. Jai had called Noel *Ima* as a joke when Addie was just a baby, but Addie had caught on quickly. Once she picked up the habit, there was no going back. Noel never seemed to mind; Addie didn't either, even when most of the other Imas in Utopia were female.

Coming to a stop at Gideon's side, I leaned against his strong body, nuzzling his chest as he wrapped an arm around me. "I figured she was with you."

"I should have known not to trust a four year old at her word," he said with a peck to my head. "Next time, I'll call to make sure."

"It's not your fault. You know how Jai gets," I said, and Jai shot me a half-hearted glare, flipping me his middle finger.

"Still." Gideon rubbed my shoulder, smiling down at me. His green eyes twinkled as he inspected my clothes, still rumpled from Noel's and my tryst in the kitchen. He bit his bottom lip, then whispered into my scalp. "You, uh, have a bit of cum on your shirt."

I glanced down in horror at the smear of semen drying on the hem of my shirt. Burying my face in Gideon's pectoral, I tucked the front of my shirt into my jeans to hide it. "Oh my God, that's embarrassing."

My face burned as Gideon chuckled. He cupped my chin and pressed a swift kiss to my mouth. "As long as you didn't do it in the kitchen."

"How was the market?" I asked, smoothly changing the subject, and Gideon frowned at me. I smiled innocently. His scowl darkened.

"Daddy?"

Little fingers circled my pinkie and tugged. Both Gideon and I looked down, finding Addie gazing up at us with wide, wet eyes. With a grunt, I heaved her up and into my arms, my ruined thigh spasming for a second. Gideon's hand at my waist tightened, steadying me.

"Yes, baby girl?" I asked as her thin arms circled my neck. Her weight was familiar, and when she laid her head on my shoulder and cuddled close, my heart seized. She smelled like honeysuckle and smoke.

"I'm sowwy," she said as her hand petted the back of my neck.

I kissed her forehead and snuggled her close. "That's okay. But next time, you tell Papa that you're going to hold Abba's hand or Ima's, especially when you're in the market or the store." Her head bobbed, and I kissed her chubby cheek. "Now, I think you need to tell Abba sorry too for lying."

Transferring her to the final parent, I stepped back, allowing Jai to pull me into him. His arms crossed over my chest, chin digging into the top of my head. I leaned back, hands hooking on his forearms as Gideon propped Addie on his hip and smoothed her curls away from her face.

"Adelaide, I'm not upset that you wanted to walk with me in the market instead of Papa, but I don't like that you lied to me. You made Papa really worried, and he scared Ima and Daddy because they thought you were lost. If you'd been honest with me, I could have found Papa or called him, and no one would have been worried. That's why it's important that you're always honest with Abba. And with Papa and Ima and Daddy too."

With a trembling lower lip, Addie nodded. "I'm sowwy, Abba."

"I forgive you, and I love you very much. So does Daddy and Papa and Ima. We get worried because we love you and we want you safe."

"Mad?" she asked tentatively.

"No, dearest one, we're not mad." Gideon kissed the tip of her nose, and she giggled. All four of us sighed at the wonderful sound. We were such saps for her. "Now, how about we use the fresh fruit we bought to make smoothies. What do you think?"

She clapped her hands and shrieked in delight. "Yes, yes! Smoodies!"

As she wiggled and writhed, Gideon set her down, and she took off toward the house. Noel gave chase, growling in a way that made her squeal. Gideon chuckled and followed after them, leaving Jai to fall into step beside me as I gimped along.

Without warning, Jai scooped me into his arms bridal style, and I screeched. "What are you—put me down!"

"No." He dipped his head and blew a raspberry into my neck. I squawked unattractively and struggled in his arms, but he always had been and always would be stronger than me. His lips puckered against my throat, his teasing turning into tender kisses. "I am sorry," he said. "I was a total asshole for saying that you don't care."

Looping my arm around his neck, I nodded. "Yeah, you were."

He pulled back just enough to touch our foreheads and gaze into my eyes. "I'm sorry. I love you."

"I love you too, and I forgive you. You were upset."

"Doesn't give me an excuse to be a dick."

He had me there. "True. But I'm sure you'll figure out a way to make it up to me."

A dark eyebrow arched. "Oh?" He shifted me in his grasp until my legs were wrapped around his waist, his hands on my butt. "And how exactly do you want me to make it up to you?"

I grinned. "Surprise me."

A deep fire flickered in his dark eyes, and he squeezed my butt. "I'm sure I can think of something." Another giggled shriek sounded from the kitchen as Jai carried me into the entry, and he grimaced. "Later, though."

"I'm a patient guy," I said, and he set me down with a smack to my butt.

"Yeah, sure you are."

With a kiss full of sinful promise, Jai led me to the kitchen where Gideon was plugging in the blender. Addie sat on a stool as Noel ran a soapy washcloth over the kitchen island counter where, less than half an hour ago, we'd had sex. I tried not to blush as Noel caught my eye and winked.

Once everything was sanitized, Gideon spread the fruit option on the island so Addie could make her choice. As Gideon mixed the smoothies, Noel and Addie giggled and whispered conspiratorially. Jai hooked an arm around my neck, his lips puckering against my scalp. And I smiled.

"Are you happy?" Jai asked into my hair, and I nodded, squeezing his arm.

"I've never been happier," I said, and it was the complete and utter truth.

The End

TRANSLATIONS

Abba - Father

Ahuvi - My love

Ani ohev otcha - I love you

Ani l'dodi v'dodi li - I am my beloved's and my beloved is mine

Chaim sheli - My life

Ima - Mother

Kapara - My hope, my redemption

Neshama sheli - My soul

ABOUT NIKOLE KNIGHT

Nikole Knight is a born and bred Hoosier living in a top-secret location in Europe. She's the lone female in the house, unless you count the dog, and she writes love in all its forms.

When she isn't busy adulting, Nikole can be found in her writing nook, typing away as her fingers turn to nubs.

For exclusive content, updates, and information on all things Knight, sign up for Nikole's newsletter <u>here</u> or join her Facebook group: <u>Nikole's Knights</u>.

BOOKS BY NIKOLE KNIGHT

Fire & Brimstone Universe:

The Complete Scrolls
Revelations

Sacrifice

Illusion

Betrayal

Redemption

Elysium

The Complete Series Box Set

Short Stories
Scrolls from the Archives: A Short Story Collection

<u>The Foxxxy Gentlemen's Club:</u>

Luca
Christian
Angel

<u>Far From Ruined Trilogy:</u>

Every Broken Thing
Every Hidden Truth
Every Mended Heart

<u>Stand-Alone Novels & Short Stories:</u>

A Human's Guide to Wooing an Asexual Incubi
The Death Games
The Night We Met
Night Skies and Galaxy Leggings

Audiobooks by Nikole Knight

The Complete Fire & Brimstone Scrolls
Narrated by Kirt Graves

The Foxxxy Gentlemen's Club: Christian
Narrated by John York

The Foxxxy Gentlemen's Club: Luca
Narrated by John York

<u>A Human's Guide to Wooing an Asexual</u> <u>Incubi</u>
Narrated by Jason Chacon